The Tortured Earth

A NOVEL OF THE RUSSIAN FRONT

By GERT LEDIG

Translated by MERVYN SAVILL

HENRY REGNERY COMPANY

CHICAGO · 1956

C.2

HR

As the corporal stuffed the loose dirt

into the exhaust pipe of the tank he realized how

futile his effort was, but it gave him

enormous satisfaction anyway—somehow he

was striking back. The runner kept fingering

the leaflet in his pocket, the leaflet

guaranteeing him safety if he deserted to

the enemy, and wondering in his terror what to do.

The counter offensive for hill 608 had failed,

and the company was almost totally wiped out.

The major had ordered the attack

knowing it to be hopeless, in a mood of

revenge, for he had just learned his wife

and daughter had been killed.

With the enormous power of a human soul

profoundly outraged by the calculated inhumanity

of war, Gert Ledig has pounded out the most

shattering novel of World War II.

The Tortured Earth

A NOVEL OF THE RUSSIAN FRONT

Prologue

THE CORPORAL could not turn in his grave because he didn't have one. Three versts from Podrowa and about forty south of Leningrad he had been caught by a salvo of rockets and flung into the air. With his hands blown off and his head downwards he now hung in a bare stump which had once been a tree.

The sergeant, crawling about the ground with shrapnel in his belly, didn't know where his machine gunner had gone. He never thought of looking up. He had troubles enough of his own.

The other two men of his crew ran off without bothering about their sergeant. If anyone had asked them later why they didn't try to get the corporal down from the tree, they would have called him crazy, and quite rightly. The corporal, thank God, was already dead. Half an hour later, what was left of the tree was sawed off by machine-gun fire and his mutilated body fell to the ground anyway. Meanwhile he had lost another foot. The jagged sleeves of his field jacket were clotted with blood. When he did reach the earth he was only half a man.

With the sergeant's machine-gun nest wiped out, the

narrow log-road was cleared for the shock troops of Lieutenant Vyacheslav Dotoev. He waved to the tank which was careening in front of his men, most of them rounded up from the Stalin Academy of Art. There was a rattle of tracks and a moment later all that remained of the German corporal had been flattened out. The students from the Stalin Academy could not even rifle his pockets.

After the caterpillar tracks had lumbered over the corporal, a fighter pilot threw a burst into the mass of rags, flesh and blood.

Then, finally, the corporal was at rest.

For a month he stank—until only his bones lay scattered about in the grass. He never made it to a grave. Two days after the corporal lost his hands, the captain signed a report of his death.

The sergeant major prepared it.

A number of these reports had come in together. The captain signed seven of them that day. The sergeant major always stuck to regulations—he arranged the reports according to the ranks of the missing men. The report on the corporal's death was signed after the report on the sergeant. In this way the sergeant major brought a certain order into the matter. Things like this made him indispensable at company headquarters. He had no idea that his reports followed the order of fate. Only the dead corporal could have reported that the first part of the salvo had hit his sergeant and that he himself had not been flung into the air until a second later. But the corporal could no longer make any report. Besides, he had no hands to raise to his

2

steel helmet in salute. Thus, by an inscrutable turn everything was put on the right track.

When it came to signing his sergeant's reports the captain had broken himself of asking whether the man was
married or whether his mother was still alive. Nobody
would ask it, either, if one day they should write a report
on his own death. He realized that it was no use, anyway,
to ask such a question. It didn't matter to him. He wanted
to live just as all the others wanted to live. By now he
thought it was far better not to be a hero, only to stay alive.

Whenever the opportunity arose—and one arose almost
every night—he tried to strike a bargain with God whom he
had forgotten for ten years. According to the heaviness of
the bombardment which fell on their dugout he offered
God a hand or foot in exchange for his life. When the
Russians stormed the corduroy road he had offered God
both his feet. But he never offered his eyesight and never
mentioned it in his prayers.

So far God had shown no particular inclination to do
business with him. Possibly God was taking revenge for
the ten years of neglect. It was difficult for the captain to
come to terms with Him after so long. In these surround-
ings it was almost ridiculous to attempt a conversation
with God in the manner of a college professor. It was much
better to approach Him as a company commander, but it
was always difficult to seal a bargain for one's own destiny. In this role the captain had to put his request at the
end of the prayer. He could only stress the importance of

his requests by showing himself ready for some particular sacrifice. To beg God humbly for his life only entered his mind much later—when he could only wait in his dugout and see whether the Russian outside would fling a hand grenade into it. After ten years in the role of professor he did not realize that God was not obliged to grant such a prayer.

A lance corporal, without wasting a thought on God, had clawed the earth so long with his nails that his fingers hung in bloody shreds. He then had calmly watched the flies and mosquitos settle on the raw flesh instilling in his body certain poisons he needed to carry out his plan. A few days later with badly infected hands, a high temperature and other symptoms of sickness difficult to diagnose, he reported at the casualty clearing station. The lance corporal had chosen the simplest way. He had not bothered his head about any relationship with God. For twenty years he had never set foot in a church. Later he felt no need to do such a thing and God did not meet him a second time.

But these were things which had nothing to do with the report on the missing corporal. The man whom that concerned was the runner from company headquarters. He stuffed the sheet of paper carelessly in his pocket together with his pipe and the remains of a packet of sunflower seeds which he had taken from a Russian prisoner. His stay in the headquarters dugout did not last very long.

The road to battalion headquarters was really not a

road nor did it offer the least security. Several times a day the runner ran for his life along a kind of footworn path. He blamed this wrestle with death largely on the sergeant major who was constantly sending important reports to battalion headquarters so as to give his presence in the company dugout some justification. Several times a day he had to see that the captain did not get the notion to send him up to the front lines with a detachment. It did not disturb the sergeant major in the least that sooner or later the runner's children would become orphans.

The runner was terrified of the first hundred yards from company headquarters. A Russian mortar was trained on the dugout and regularly spattered the little parapet with shrapnel. No one ever lingered there for more than a few seconds and got away with it, for the Russian snipers shot down any moving target. Both the runner and the sergeant major knew this.

Each time the sergeant major sent him out on a trivial errand the runner made up his mind that one day he would take his revenge. He could never have killed an enemy in cold blood but the next time they went over the top he would certainly shoot his sergeant major in the back. He loathed him. The heart lay half a hand's breadth below the left shoulder blade. A certain knowledge of anatomy was essential in his profession and the runner was proud of the fact. Each time he sped across the hundred yards he thought of this murder. Then he reached the cover of undergrowth and once more he was safe. It would be pure chance if he ran into machine-gun fire here.

5

Things only really looked hopeless when he started to climb the hill. It looked exactly like a moon landscape. The only thing he would not have found on the moon was the giant steel mast of the high tension pylon. A few of the struts were still upright although bent by direct hits, but the mighty concrete base had resisted shells of all calibres. Not far from the pylon was a soldier's grave, which must have dated from the time of the advance. A low wooden fence ran around the pile of earth but the cross with the soldier's name had been destroyed by a shell. The men in the company called it "The Grave of the Unknown Soldier."

The hill with the high tension pylon would have been an ideal observation post for the whole sector, but installing a range finder on this ploughed up earth would have been as futile as sticking a mirror in a revolving concrete mixer.

While the runner glided over the hill like a ghost he found himself in another world. Here the laws of gravity did not apply. He flew rather than ran among the whizzing shells. Every thought was a waste of time. A cold wind blew over the bare earth and the realm of ghosts had received him. He was chased by the riders of the Apocalypse, with death in the lead on a pallid horse. No trees, no bushes, no grass, nothing but torn up sandy earth and here and there stagnant water in the shell holes.

And yet men lived up there—a corporal and two privates. One night with their hands and a short handled spade they had dug a hole under the concrete. Now they lay there on the watch waiting for the inevitable hour to come when the company in the trenches behind them would be wiped out. Then they were supposed to run up to the approaching steel monsters and, with trembling hands and, in all probability, lead in their bellies, hang the death-dealing explosive charges on the tanks as they passed. Hour after hour, day after day, they waited for this moment, always in the hope that it would never come. The concrete block rocked and creaked over their heads; sand trickled down the walls into their hole. Even if the tanks did not appear the moment would certainly come when the concrete would collapse and bury them. The foxhole kept growing larger from the blast of the nearby explosions. Each day it grew more obvious; sooner or later the concrete base supporting the weight of the steel pylon would squash the air bubble below it. Nevertheless they could not leave it. Should they go and lie in a shell hole in order to be killed an hour later?

The corporal and his two men lived in a prison. They huddled close together with canisters of dynamite between their stinking bodies. From dented mess tins they drank a filthy black liquid brought to them as coffee—colored water that tasted of tin and chicory. On their tongues they could feel the sand which continually trickled down from the roof into the mess kits. Sometimes they undressed and squatted like naked hermits in their hole searching their uniforms for small fat glittering vermin. Each day they waited longingly for their daily ration of alcohol. They gulped it down quickly and from day to day grew more

7

surprised to find how sober they remained. When they had to relieve nature they did it on the short spade or in old tins, throwing the excrement outside. In this way they did not have to risk their lives unnecessarily. Sometimes the turds fell back into the hole. They were like spectres. Their hair began to grow over their collars. They were greasy and dusty, but they went on listening, trying to hear one particular noise above the wail of the shells, whether they were asleep, smoking or drinking. They were waiting for the rattle of the Russian tank tracks.

A few times a day and occasionally at night the runner came to their foxhole. He was their contact with the world, which for them had shrunk to half a mile of front line. If he said anything that sounded like "relief" his remarks were repeated and gave food for conversation for hours or days on end. And the days went by. In the army of forgotten men this antitank squad was a cipher. They shook hands with each new reinforcement the runner brought up the line and secretly wished for his death. He increased the fighting strength of the company and sounded the knell of their hopes for relief.

They rummaged unceremoniously in the runner's leather dispatch case and in the half light deciphered with gruesome satisfaction the list of the missing and dead. They figured out just how long it would take until the infantry company was reduced to a mere handful of men. Then it would be taken out of the front line.

This was the only object in the runner's case that interested them. The front-line Intelligence Report which he brought daily from battalion headquarters to the company was not worth reading. The performance report of the new machine gun, which the sergeant major had composed for the divisional staff only brought forth a compassionate smile. The lance corporal lit his pipe with it. In this way he made sure that no safe post at battalion headquarters would be given to the sergeant major.

The lance corporal always kept a check on the information reports when they referred to jobs behind the lines. He was careful to nip any such ambitions in the bud. A request from the sergeant major to the major vanished into thin air in the antitank squad's dugout. The sergeant major's name stood on the list of men for special leave. By the time the list reached battalion, "temporarily irreplaceble" in the lance corporal's handwriting stood below his name. Just as tragedy is only one step removed from comedy, so knavery rubbed elbows with horror in this louse-ridden cesspool under the hill of death.

The runner left the foxhole. Before turning away he said offhandedly that if he were still alive he would look in on them again on the way back. He need not have said this: his overstrained lungs forced him to make use of this halfway house. He spoke only so he would not succumb to fear. A prayer would have done just as well.

Once more he was running across the cratered landscape. Steel-nosed shells twittered around him like birds. The fountain of earth flung up by one of them swallowed

him and spat him out again. His fingers clutched the leather dispatch case. He hopped through shell holes and
trenches and finally landed, trembling feverishly, behind
the railway embankment. Although he was again in the
front line the rocks gave a certain amount of protection.
Shells streaked across the sky like rockets from horizon to
horizon. None of them deviated from their path. He could
hear rifle fire but there was no need to fear it. The rails on
the embankment seemed to be the boundary. Only the
splattering mortar shells kept him going at a fast pace.
Even here he was not altogether safe from a stray hit.
The five-hundred-yard railway line, however, had one
advantage: the loneliness, in which fear was more acute,
was temporarily overcome. Every fifty yards a grimy figure
leaned against the embankment. Although these figures
rarely turned around, because they didn't dare take their
eyes off no man's land, their mere presence was something
of a comfort. This treacherous feeling of security lasted
until he reached the vicinity of the dressing station dugout.
The sight of corpses and rigid bodies destroyed all illusions. It began with those who had been brought there
with loss of blood or torn off limbs.

Reluctantly the stretcher-bearers had to admit that the
burdens they were carrying on the canvas were already
dead. They pulled the birch poles out of the stretcher
sheets, turned the corpse out and left it lying near the aid
station dugout. Thanks to the constant bombardment they
could carry the wounded only at night and for them the
night lasted until dawn. They were in a hurry to carry am-

munitions or soggy bread up to the front line on the same stretchers.

The runner saw the casualties lying there. Those with stomach wounds still writhed with pain. If he could not distinguish them by their doubled-up bodies, he could at least do so by their naked bellies. They belonged in the category of the doomed. To bring them in was a futile gesture which one could not refuse them as long as they were still conscious. Or their animal screams furnished a reason for them to be picked up. But everything depended upon the circumstances and these were seldom alike.

For example, the railway line a few miles away was once more in service. In the divisional sector the front line—or what was marked on the general staff map as the front line—started from the railway. The tracks ran in an easterly direction. Where they left the firing zone of the German medium batteries the Russians were using them to bring up supplies. A party was given the task of temporarily crippling this system by blowing up the rails before the company captured the high ground. This party (it was a bare eight weeks before) had been led by a lieutenant. He and his men thought it should be a job for the air force. The sergeant major on the other hand maintained that only the general staff was in a position to judge this and that he himself had the greatest confidence in this vital strategic foray. This was the usual gist of his remarks when he had to get a patrol together. He always ended with the assurance that he regretted his duties would not allow him to take part in the show. Meller, a sapper, was the only

one who dared give the sergeant major a cynical grin.
Meller invariably invited the sergeant to come along with
them all the same. For this reason Meller was always de-
tailed for every dangerous job. The first time the sergeant
major found a word of recognition for Meller was when
he was no longer among the living. After the railway line
had been blown up six miles behind the Russian lines
Meller was hit in the belly. The bullet entered from behind, an inch and a half below his belt and just to the left
of his spine. It left the body almost in a straight line to the
left of his navel. No one had time to examine the wound.
Meller had a burnt hole in the back and front of his tunic
and could no longer fill in as the second stretcher bearer
for the dead lieutenant. The corporal had only a second to
make up his mind whether he should leave the lieutenant's
body or take it back. He did not have to decide whether
he should dump the superfluous ammunition boxes so as to
have another stretcher bearer for the wounded sapper—
Meller said that he could still walk. Two hundred yards
further on the ammunition boxes and their bearer fell out
of their own accord: the man was blown sky high after
stepping on a land mine. Then two more men were wounded and the situation became critical. The corporal shot
the rounds from an excess cartridge belt into the air and
flung the belt and the weapon into a puddle. Meller had
fallen back and the NCO was compelled to remain behind
with him. Turning round he fired his submachine gun into
the brown ranks of attacking Russians behind him. Once
they reached the marsh they were safe from further losses

for they now had cover in the undergrowth. Now they had to find the path which the patrol had taken the day before to slip unnoticed through the advance Russian positions. This took the corporal only about half an hour. In the meantime Meller was insisting that he could still walk unaided. They had been walking along the path through the marsh for nearly half a mile when the NCO discovered an enemy machine-gun post ahead. The noose had tightened around the survivors of the patrol. With a wry smile on his lips Meller volunteered to wipe it out. A nod from the NCO gave him permission to rush with two live hand grenades at the surprised machine-gun crew. When the surviving six men of the party sprang from cover after the explosions they ran past the dying sapper. He lay on his back. His leg had been cut off at the thigh by machine gun fire. He might have lived long enough for some infuriated Russian to have stuck a bayonet in his chest in revenge for his dead comrades. Only the runner saw the corporal aim his revolver at the sapper's head. He never forgot the sight of the NCO who, without thinking of his own life, stood calmly saluting the dead man, but he never mentioned what he had seen. Words would have been quite inadequate. He did, however, understand why the NCO could not write the inevitable letter to Frau Meller ("A painless death. Shot through the heart"). The sergeant major wrote this letter.

So with belly wounds, too, it always depended upon the circumstances. The pile of corpses was composed of wounded men of different types. One raised his arm and legs to the sky. Another lay naked in the grass, his skin blackened by the caress of a flame thrower. The runner would have needed an hour to observe them all.

Instead, he approached the entrance to the dugout. Here the dead were separated from the living. He could not bear to see this hell of a slaughter house and he ran past with closed eyes. Nevertheless he heard the groaning and whimpering of men begging for a drop of water.

After this he could turn off left into the woods. The trees, or rather what remained of them, immediately swallowed him up. They meant cover from mortar shells, machine guns, and shrapnel. The whistling in the air above became dangerous again only when he came to the artillery positions.

As soon as he entered the wood he became a prey to his fatigue. The undergrowth and the birch trunks were silent. The footpath, strewn with Russian soldiers who had died of hunger or been shot, made no sound beneath his feet. A swarm of mosquitoes danced over a corpse lying in a stagnant pool in a clearing. A beetle in its glittering armor carried a blade of grass across his path. A circle of burnt grass, an uprooted tree and a pile of broken branches gave evidence that recently, perhaps yesterday, perhaps an hour ago, death had struck. A few rays of sunlight trickled through the leaves. The air shimmered. Half hidden by the branches a white rag warned the initiated of the presence of a minefield. Behind the runner there was a rumble as of far off thunder. The loneliness took hold of him and constricted his heart. He was constantly wait-

14

ing for some piece of treachery. There were two possibilities. One was silent like the forest and gave no warning. It lay hidden behind a tree trunk or in the tall grass. It came like a whiplash out of the undergrowth. The blow was always fatal and had the sole advantage of being over quickly. This possibility took the form of a bundle of rags and a revolver. Half crazed with hunger and tortured by the same fear as himself it lay in wait behind a tree trunk. A flash and a whiplash—perhaps a little puff of smoke. Then a brown figure would spring silently from its hiding place and bend over the dead man. From his fingers it wrenched the weapon and rummaged feverishly in his pockets. The useful and the useless disappeared in the pockets of the tattered bundle which then vanished like a ghost. Only a dead man remained whom the flies would dance over until he was found. If there were marshy ground nearby he was never found.

The other possibility ended in the same way but it announced itself. It started with the roar of an infuriated beast in the distance, a dull groaning noise unlike anything else in the world. It echoed over a few versts like a hunting cry. Twice, or three times, it roared. Then came the creaking of a badly tuned organ. Paralysis descended upon the front line. The rattle of machine guns fell silent. The snipers drew their rifles back behind the parapet. The mortar crews huddled close together and the words of command froze on the lips of the gunner officers. The runner slowed down his pace. Then all hell broke open. Countless bursts of fire slashed the woods. Nearly half a hundred shells burst in the trees or on the ground. Deafening thunder. . . . Flames, gunpowder, pieces of copper as big as fists. Earth and mud. . . . A battery with four guns, ammunition boxes, cartridges, tools and horses was hurled into the mire. An hour later it burst on a field kitchen. The driver and his mate, the cook, the provisions for sixty men, and twenty-five gallons of watery soup were strewn to the four winds. A few minutes later it wailed down on a relief company marching up to the lines—eighty men carefully smartened up, with polished boots and oiled rifles, coming from the rear lines. The forty men who reached the trenches were filthy dirty, bloodstained and demoralized. Two hours, two days, two weeks. . . . Somewhere a tank detachment was on the move preparatory to action. In the shelter of a hollow the commander assembled his troops to give them their final orders. A swish on the horizon. Five or six seconds of oppressive silence and then the shots burst out of the blue. Screams. . . . Shrapnel rained down on the empty tanks. The junior officer had great difficulty in finding enough drivers to bring back the twelve tanks with their dead crews inside. Everyone who had felt the earth shudder and seen the smoke of the explosions in the sky thanked destiny or God—each in his own fashion—that someone else had caught it and that he had been spared once more. The runner too, who had knelt down with his hands before his face, thanked his foresight. This, then, was the nature of the second possibility.

The runner hurried along the footpath with his reports and the sunflower seeds in his pocket. He still had the last half of the journey ahead of him and there was no need to hang about any longer than necessary. The droning above the trees increased in volume. The artillery batteries joined in. The forest thinned out. There were occasional paths, luxuriant undergrowth and poisonous toadstools. The foot-path came to an end and gave place to a well-beaten track which the rain had turned into a welter of mud. On one side was a burnt out *panje* cart—mouldering leather reins and the skeleton of a horse. On either side of the road were weather-beaten cardboard notices covered with mysterious signs. They indicated the whereabouts of a field telephone for a howitzer battery, so that over there in the clearing, almost underground, a flak gun could raise its long barrel to the sky. Occasionally an amateurish skull and bones warned of land mines.

Suddenly something gurgled down from the sky. The runner flung himself to the ground. The blast of an explosion swept over him. A gigantic net which he had taken for a hill of dry branches started to billow with the withered foliage. In a fountain of dust the barrel of the gun hidden beneath the net began to wobble. For a moment it stood upright before collapsing. Someone whom the shell had not hit swore at God and another called for stretcher bearers.

The runner stood up and plodded on. He thought how rare a call for a stretcher bearer had become here. The track broadened out and the ruts grew deeper. A soldier came towards him. Leather case, dusty boots, drawn features and deep-set eyes: a runner who after two hours

17

of safety was on his way back to hell. A nod, a tired answering smile and he disappeared. . . .

The runner quickened his pace to catch up with a cart that was creaking along ahead of him. It wobbled in the deep ruts. The cloud of dust which it threw up in its wake settled like a veil on the runner and he felt a furry taste on his tongue. A canvas tarpaulin covered the load in the cart, which was pulled by a sturdy horse. Only when the runner stretched out his hand to the backboard to hoist himself up did he recognize the cargo. Under the canvas, stiff hands rapped against the muddy floor and bare heads nodded to and fro. The stiff-legged travellers kicked each other in the belly. They were frozen into positions which no living man could have adopted. Two were in fraternal embrace while others grinned with distorted faces. The runner shrank back.

He squatted in the sand until the cloud of dust had disappeared around the next bend. The clatter of an approaching shell brought him to his senses. Again he came across notices, guns, and bandoliers of empty cartridges by the roadside. They were left behind. . . .

At last the field with the thistles and the damp patches which never dried up came into view and then the endless rows of beechwood crucifixes. The cartload of corpses had pulled up outside the cemetery. A number of figures with shaved heads were digging. A few of them were busy unloading the cart while others dragged a dead body through the grass.

Behind the last rows of graves he could see the village.

Squat huts, log blockhouses covered with weatherbeaten wooden shingles on both sides of the road. . . . A well, and nearby on a mast the battalion's metal flag.

The runner stumbled into the building. The adjutant was standing by the door. He saluted and took his reports from the leather dispatch case.

At this very moment the runner began to fall asleep. As in a dream he turned around, staggered back along the corridor, planted his feet like a sleep walker on the steps of the entrance. He slumped down on the wooden bench near the well. Weariness descended upon him like a black pall. From company headquarters to the battalion—orders carried out.

Chapter One

THE ADJUTANT read over the company reports in his hand. He read the names of men who no longer existed, who were now only obliterated concepts, part and parcel of the past. The losses: one machine gun—serial number unrecognizable, two bandoliers, one reserve gun barrel, one N.C.O. and seven men. There was little sense in showing these reports to the commanding officer. Life here pivoted upon himself and the C.O. The door opened and names arrived; the door shut and names disappeared. Here both life and death were given a number. These two had to see that the job was completed. He had his work to do and the C.O.'s job did not interest him in the least.

He knocked on the door, which was covered with cardboard. No one knew quite why. Perhaps to arouse respect. The door may have let in the drafts, or maybe the cardboard showed that this door led to the C.O.

The major sat at a desk covered with papers. Anyone could see how tired he was. He smelled of the musty house —a mixture of stale smoke, rotting wood, dirty linen, sweat and vermin. He had not shaved for a couple of days, perhaps a week. He looked like a corpse whose beard had continued to grow, as if he had been lying there in state for some time. His glass eye threw his face out of proportion. The living eye looked at the four legs of the table one after the other; at the four tins filled with yellow water in which dead lice swam. He wanted to see whether the lice had bred. He did it quite absentmindedly for it was a matter of indifference to him. It was a long time since he had counted the rigid bodies on the top of the water.

By the time the adjutant entered the room the major was already busy looking at other phenomena that caught his eye: a spider's web on the smooth oil-paper tablecloth, a wheel, the weights of a clock. . . . Clocks that ticked, slowly but ruthlessly shortening life's span.

While he watched them, fascinated as though they contained a secret, he felt like something drifting lifeless in the water. The stream flowed over his skin and he was swimming. It did him good. When he awoke from this reverie his pain returned—an unbearable pain which he could no longer endure. He felt as though he had borne it for an eternity. It weighed him down like lead. The words of the telegram hammered pitilessly in his brain: ANNA AND CHILD DEAD STOP BURIED UNDER DEBRIS OF HOUSE STOP BODIES UNRECOGNIZABLE STOP IMMEDIATE BURIAL.

He had lost the telegram, but the pain remained. As the major sat there alone at his table he kept on thinking: ANNA AND CHILD DEAD. He stared at the dirty walls with his mouth open not saying a word. The sweat poured down his forehead. All he could remember of Anna was that she had black hair. He could no longer remember her face. Yet they had lived together for twenty years. For twenty long years they had seen each other every day.

He had lain with her in bed and kissed her on the lips every morning but he could remember only one thing: she had black hair. On the other hand he had a picture of his child taken one summer's day in the garden. Flowers in the sun. . . . A pair of bright eyes smiling at him. The camera had caught them. Now the child was dead.

The major giggled to himself and looked out through one of the broken window panes. The runner lay there asleep on the bench. The sun was setting and the gnats were swarming in the air. Everything was just as he had expected it to be—the street, the village pump and the fiery disc of the sun on the horizon. A soldier in conspicuously white drill passed and spat contemptuously in the sand. Everyone he knew was still alive. Only his child had to die, as though he had owed a reckoning. Now it had been paid. Unexpected and ruthless. That was gratitude, justice.

He turned around and gave an order: "Tell the runner to come in."

"Yes, sir," replied the adjutant. A draft of air lifted three sheets of typing paper from the table; they floated slowly to the ground.

As the major picked them up he again looked out through the dirty glass of the window pane. He saw how the runner, awakened by the adjutant, stood up, slipped past the window, disappeared from view for a moment, and appeared suddenly before him in the office.

"At ease," said the major, but only from habit. The runner stood there slack and undisciplined without having bothered to stand at attention.

"Everything in order?" asked the major. All the while he went on thinking of his dead child. A misfortune whose consequences could not have been foreseen. Something which he had forgotten always came into the picture.

"Yes, sir," replied the runner.

"And on the logpath?"

The adjutant interrupted. "Untenable, sir." He went over and stood next to the runner. For a moment they stared at each other. Two men coming to an understanding with each other. In silence, without uttering a word.

The major grew angry. "Very interesting."

"Yes," replied the adjutant, staring at his finger nails. "An exposed point. No one is to blame. I'll pass on the necessary information at once to the division," he said, suddenly looking up.

Outside on the street a heavy truck lumbered past making the earth tremble and raising the dust. A piece of glass fell out of the window pane. It tinkled on the ground and broke.

"The artillery regiment is probably being reinforced," said the adjutant.

"Which one?" The runner's question rang out like a pistol shot.

"Don't speak until you're spoken to," ordered the major angrily. "Give me the map, please." He turned to the adjutant. His second in command rummaged about among the papers on the table. Beneath his tunic he wore a shirt with cuffs. Both cuffs were soiled. They had grey rims around the edges.

The runner looked at the map with feigned indifference and heard the adjutant's voice saying: "At least we owe that to our men." He pointed vaguely to the table and no one was quite certain what he meant.

"Owe it to them?" repeated the major slowly. He looked at the runner and shook his head.

"I'm convinced," the adjutant insisted in a businesslike manner, "that our viewpoint will be accepted."

"What the hell do I care?"

"I beg your pardon," said the adjutant giving a nervous little cough.

"I said, what the hell do I care," repeated the major aggressively. He joined his hands together and felt an unhealthy moistness as though he were feverish. He could of course have sent for the doctor and for a moment he toyed with the idea. He could easily convince the doctor that he was sick. Then to his annoyance he thought: perhaps I really am sick.

"You can smoke if you like," the adjutant said to the runner. "We don't mind." He was very much the man of the world who felt quite at home anywhere—quite indifferent to what happened.

"Thank you, sir."

The runner carefully filled his pipe but when the operation was finally completed he did not light it. He did not want to miss anything. A bluebottle which had been buzzing round the stove started to fly towards the window. It banged against the glass and fell to the floor. Below the floor boards they could hear a noise like the scuttling around of rats.

"What were we just talking about?"

"Whether to launch a counter-attack or not," replied the adjutant coolly. He held the question up to the major as though he were displaying a picture at an auction. Going. . . . going. The adjutant had already made his bid. No counter-attack, no unnecessary sacrifice.

The runner stared hard at the window and took in every word.

"You know the order don't you?" asked the major.

"What order?"

"The positions must be held. Any break-through by the enemy has to be mopped up by a counter-attack."

"Of course, of course," replied the adjutant apologetically. There were hundreds of orders. No soldier could disobey an order, but he could forget it.

The major thought of his child. It was just only if other people received similar telegrams. "I must have satisfaction," he thought. His hands were now even damper, as though he had dipped them in water. One can numb a pain if he takes revenge and now he wanted to take his revenge. "There are no exceptions to the order," he said and noticed that the runner was staring at his glass eye as though he expected to see it fall to the ground at any moment.

"But, Major!" The adjutant pointed to the map on the

table. His finger followed a black line which led through the marshes. "The logpath is worthless. There's no embankment. Just a path made out of fir trunks." Then he pointed to a red cross. "This machine gun is in a ridiculously exposed position." The major did not have to listen to any more. He knew what was coming: the futility of this post, the narrow path through no-man's land. Thin tree trunks merely laid side by side. No direct contact with the rest of the company and between the tree trunks the oozing marsh. The Russian M.G. was trained on the path. An artificial camouflage of branches hid it from view but did not interfere with the field of fire. Exploding projectiles rained down constantly on this single line of communication. The position itself: a tangle of uprooted trees, stumps and bare bushes. No shell holes—the marshy ground immediately closed over any hits. It was a miracle that the group had held out so long.

"In addition to this the company has had serious losses. Every man is urgently needed. How can you justify a counter-attack?" concluded the adjutant removing his hand from the map. He waited for a reply and now the runner began to realize what was coming. It was hard for the major not to see how things stood. To keep from it, he once more had to think of his child. His only child had been killed and he must not forget it. He wished he could say as much to his subordinate. Why should it happen to me? What have I done to deserve it? I never had a house built for me in French style like the artillery colonel. You can see it from the window. It stands just over there. The gunners live in mud holes. I don't lay out an extravagant officers' mess with candles and white china. I don't keep a mistress. I don't take official trips behind the lines. No luxuries, only the worries about the battalion. I never wanted this campaign. I'm a civilian and my child has been murdered. My role as a guardian angel is now over. . . .

"Can you justify that?" repeated the adjutant.

"We have replacements," shouted the major. "Enough to bring the company up to strength."

"Yes, sir."

The runner cringed and turned pale. He remembered his hope that they would all die. Crumble to pieces. That one after the other would come back to the rear wounded or dead. Until the rest would have to be relieved.

"Enough replacements to bring them up to fighting strength," said the major in his normal voice.

The adjutant smiled. "Replacements!" He shrugged his shoulders contemptuously. "The boys have no experience. They should remain here and gradually get experience."

He'll go on trying to persuade me, thought the major, until I'm sitting alone once more at the table watching the weights of the clock and hearing it tick. It would comfort me if other people also had to make sacrifices. I must hear that they have—otherwise I'll lose my mind. He clung to his decision and barked: "Carry out my orders!"

"Counter-attack then across the logpath?"

Outside in the street the heavy truck returned, skidding all over the road. The walls trembled and then silence returned.

"I wanted. . . ." The major looked at his riding boots with his good eye.

"Sir?" The adjutant's voice seemed to be asking what he wanted.

"Oh, it doesn't matter." In order to gain time the major turned to the runner. "How strong is the enemy?" A ridiculous question. The adjutant made no comment and the runner merely said: "No one knows."

"Hmmm!" The major could not understand why he no longer felt inclined to take the responsibility. Until then everything had seemed so clear. His grief now made everything seem diffused: compassion, worries, the table with the tin cans in which the dead lice were swimming; the clay oven on which the Kolkhoz peasant had left behind a bundle of rags; the door with the leather hinge straps through which the adjutant had come with the telegram; the misfortunes and the destruction. Why can't I remember *her?* he thought. Something was wrong. You don't forget a person with whom you have lived for twenty years. The telegram—such a blow. You either fall on your knees and pray, become a penitent and a fool. Or you strike back. I'm going to strike back, he thought. Everyone will do penance for the child—the runner, the company in the key position, the whole world. And yet he felt something holding him back as though he wanted to leave a door open for escape. There was always a little cowardice remaining. "Copy out the divisional order," he commanded.

Now he knew what he had to do and it was comparatively simple. The adjutant carried out his orders and he, too, appeared to understand. He copied the order word for word in block letters on the paper, while the runner looked on.

Then he handed his C.O. the sheet of paper:

"Enemy break-through must be mopped up by a counter-attack."

"Good!" said the major handing the slip of paper to the runner. "Take thirty replacements up to the line, and this memorandum."

"Yes, sir." Holding the piece of paper up to the light the runner suddenly asked: "Is this a communication or an order?" The major ignored him. Turning to the adjutant he said: "Have the men fall in!"

The door banged and he could hear the adjutant's footsteps disappearing in the distance.

"Shall I wait outside?" asked the runner.

The major did not reply but went over to the window and stared at the cracks in the pane, which was held together with gummed paper. They were cracks which ran almost vertically and then suddenly shot away to one side. Their direction was unpredictable and seemed to be a matter of pure chance.

He stared at the village, and the pump loomed like a gallows against the sky. The sun was sinking behind the trees in the forest. It would soon be dusk. He felt pleased that he had struck a blow back at life. Now everything would be far easier, for he now had to make life and death decisions.

"May I make a personal request, sir?" said a voice. The major had forgotten that the runner was still standing there.

"What is it?" he asked. His back was still turned to the runner and he went on looking through the broken windowpane.

"I'd like. . . ." He boggled and started afresh. "I'd like. . . . It's only a question. Could you release me from duty?" he asked.

The major did not stir. No one had ever asked him such a question.

"Since we've been holding this position," the runner went on hastily, "I don't know how many days it is, but I've been to and fro at least a hundred times. I'm certainly no coward but I can't stand it any more. I can't stand it. . . ." He spoke very quickly. The feverish melody of the route rang through his voice: "I don't know what I'm doing. The high ground . . . it's like a rifle range. I'm the target and everyone shoots at me. And the woods with the wounded and the dead. I'm tired. Sometimes I think my lungs are going to burst."

The major drummed with his fingers on the windowpane. "Do you think it's any better with the company in the trench?"

"Yes, yes," said the runner loudly as though he were afraid the major would not hear. "There at least I can dig myself in. I won't have to run through the mortar fire. From here back to the trench is the worst. Please release me from duty, sir!"

I know all about it, thought the major. One never gets used to it. It's like diving from a great height into shallow water. One can put up with swimming but what about the dive

"You're not telling me anything new," he said. His voice sounded indifferent. He refused to be put out of his stride either by himself or by the man standing on the other side of the table.

The runner was not satisfied. "It's unfair," he said.

The major noticed the replacements coming from their huts in the village. One of them was already standing by the well. A red greasy face with protruding teeth. No self confidence. Only an impudent manner. The runner would lead him to the slaughter house. The voice behind the major said: "It would be only fair if we did it on a daily roster." Fair, thought the major. Was it fair to kill a child?

"Or at least weekly!" added the runner.

The major realized that the subject did not really interest him. He became evasive: "I can't bother my head about everything, you know."

"The captain said you had given the order that I should carry on."

"My order? He can choose another man any time he likes."

"Yes, sir. But he says, 'an order is an order.'"

The runner became importunate and went on speaking as though nothing existed apart from him. "I'll have a word with the captain," said the major. He still did not change his position. A little group of men had formed near the well. The adjutant was calling the roll. The replacements were busy with their packs. Too much gear. They'd only need a fraction of it and they wouldn't need that for long. Behind his back the runner made a movement. Perhaps he had drawn closer to the window. The major did not care. His fingers kept drumming on the window pane. Two strong and two weak taps. Always the same rhythm.

The runner cleared his throat.

"Anything else?" asked the major. He should have dismissed the man when the adjutant left.

"I can't return to the front line."

The drumming ceased.

"I'm at the end of my rope. I'm sick."

"Sick?" said the major turning around. This obviously was a barefaced lie.

"I can't move my legs any more. I've got terrible arthritis. Somebody else must take the report and the men up to the line." He had laid the piece of paper with the text of the divisional order on the table and clenched his fists—as if he were hiding something in his hands. His face and the baked clay oven seemed to be made of the same material. He fell silent as the major stared at him.

"Get out!"

The runner did not stir. He could hear snatches of orders given by the adjutant at the well.

"Pick up the report!"

The runner stretched out his hand for the paper. It was not genuine obedience, merely an automatic movement. The major saw his grey face and the tears in his eyes. The runner turned on his heel and went out without a word.

The voice behind the table had gone and the major swayed a little as he went over once more to the window. The runner could weep. The replacements were arranging themselves into a marching column. The adjutant raised his hand. The runner came up, wiping his eyes. A few men laughed in embarrassment. The runner merely shook his head. Through the dirty window the scene looked like a film. The sound track had broken. It was all silent. The runner had wept. Was it with rage or something else? Now the voices started up again. "Route step! Forward march!" ordered the adjutant. The order seemed to come out of a ravine. The runner set off along the village street with the column slouching along behind him. The men, the well, everything swam before his eyes. Why couldn't *he* weep too? Tears were supposed to be a relief. The major went on staring at the window pane and the glass reflected an alien distorted face. His own face.

Chapter Two

THE RUNNER and the replacements left the village. Their leather equipment squeaked. As they passed the last village huts a horse neighed. The cemetery was deserted. The cart with the corpses had disappeared. There was no trace of the disquieting figures.

The column marched behind the runner in silence. The front line, enclosed in the gloominess of the woods ahead, was also silent. Night spread slowly over the horizon. At dusk the front always fell silent for a while in order to prepare for the night. The runner knew this. He brought his left hand down sharply on a fly which had accompanied him all the way from the village. His right hand was still clenched tight, holding the paper he had purloined from the major's table.

The report for the company had been stuck into his pocket. Later he would throw it away. A field kitchen stood by the roadside. The relief driver was putting new fuel into the stove. Some burning embers fell out. The cauldron lid stood open. It was steaming and smelt of nothing.

The forest threw itself across the road like a threatening adversary. But then the tree trunks receded. Only a few trailing branches of undergrowth tried to clutch the runner, brushing his shoulders. He opened his fist and wanted to smooth out the paper. He looked cautiously around.

One of the men had fallen out and was trying to catch up with the single-file column which the soldiers had now formed.

The runner crumpled the paper in his hand again for it was not yet dark enough. Soon there would be the tree with the hanged man. He crossed to the other side of the path. The soldiers behind him made no effort to follow. They stayed on their side of the road and would come upon it with a shock. The runner smiled with malice.

The corpse of the hanged man swayed as if it had been fished out of the water on a long line. It was already too dark to see his face. He had been hanged only a week before; his predecessor had been a commissar and this one was only a private soldier. When parties of them were found in the woods they were shot; stragglers were hanged. They seemed to know this. Most of them kept the last bullet for themselves. That shortened the procedure. The lead man jumped to one side in terror. He had almost touched the corpse. The runner giggled. The others had now been warned and made their way carefully around the dead man. The first corpse! What an experience!

It grew darker and darker. The sky became blue black. A telegrapher's key tapped in the undergrowth but the runner could not read the message. Noises came from the gun positions in the forest. He took the report out of his pocket, tore off a strip and let it flutter to the ground.

The *panje* cart with the mouldering leather straps loomed up in their path like a ghost. No one had seen the strip of paper fall to the ground. He would soon be rid of the rest. Again and again in the darkness the little pieces of the report fluttered to the ground, into oblivion. That was all part of his plan. Soon he had only a tiny piece left. He rolled it between his fingers and flipped it away. A stray bullet whirred dully through the tree tops and came to rest in one of the trunks. The front line seemed to wake up.

The soldier behind him had at last caught up. He was panting as though in addition to his tent sheet and rifle he had been carrying a box of ammunition.

"I'm a baker," he said.

A string of tracer bullets crackled in the branches. The runner put on the steel helmet which until then he had carried at his belt. The voice at his side fell silent but after a while it repeated: "I'm a baker."

"Yes," said the runner.

"I wanted to get in with the army bakery," the voice went on.

"Would have been nice," replied the runner. He thought of bread, of warm newly-baked bread but he was not hungry. He thought of starched aprons, a tiled bakery and of clean flour dust.

"At home I've got a bakery and my own mill," the voice continued. Then, in self pity, "I've been cheated!"

"We've all been cheated," said the runner. His voice was drowned by the whistle and hiss of a shell which exploded in the wood.

"Let's get out of here!" shouted the runner but the men had already flung themselves to the ground. The baker had followed suit.

"On your feet!" roared the infuriated runner. Maybe it's just as well, he thought—they seem more at home on their bellies anyway. A minute went by, then they scrambled unwillingly to their feet and continued on their way.

"A bakery and a mill," repeated the voice at his side. A parachute flare blossomed over the forest. The harsh light came down through the torn treetops. For half a minute they walked on in the unearthly glare.

The runner turned and looked at the owner of the voice: a row of protruding teeth and a stupid face. It was only a glimpse. Then night again drew its curtain.

"I'll make it up to you," said the voice unsteadily. "A tip from you . . . I'm sure you know someone who can be spoken to. I belong in the bakery. Everyone should serve where he is most useful." The last phrase was full of cloying persuasion. "I don't know anybody," said the runner with a gesture of disgust. He noticed that he still had the paper from the major's desk clutched tightly in his fist. "Better fall back. We mustn't stick close together now because it's getting dangerous." He wanted to be alone. The shadow fell back obediently. Now he had time to think and could smooth out the paper. The major wouldn't miss one of these leaflets—they were collected in his office only to be destroyed. He knew the contents of it by heart. A truck barred their passage. Wounded men were being taken aboard. He stumbled over a stretcher. Someone swore. The paper slipped out of his hand and it took him a long time to find it again.

The column closed up and one of the men bumped into him. Others shouted: "Runner! Runner!"

He got them into line again and now he was breathless. For safety's sake he stuck the leaflet in his pocket. If there were a checkup he could say that he carried it only in case of danger. Naturally this was also forbidden but it was not such a serious crime. The leaflets came by the thousands, from nowhere. He himself had never seen any plane, but they must come out of the air. Sometimes they hung in the treetops or on the wooden shingles of the village huts. Most of them were strewn over the marsh where no one could collect them. The leaflets were sometimes pink, sometimes blue. The text was always the same.

COME OVER TO US, COMRADE! THIS PASS GUARANTEES YOU LIFE AND FREEDOM! On the back were explanations in Russian characters. He could not decipher them but a man in the company had translated them. It did not sound too bad. "Whoever produces this pass is a deserter. He has a claim to privileged treatment, life, freedom and return home after the war." No one in the company really believed it, including the runner. Nevertheless most of them carried one of the passes. This one had come from the major's table. The counterattack on the logpath could take place without him.

The business with the report was finished. No one would find the scraps of paper. Another flare burst in the sky. Through the roof of leaves the runner watched it sink. He wondered how far they still had to go and then suddenly he was in the shadow of the railway embankment. A machine gun rattled. It was as though the embankment had been waiting just for him. As if to orders, the nearest machine gun fired and was followed by a second. Bullets ran along the rails like a burning fuse, hissing and crackling, churning up the ground. The railway line seemed to be shaking with fever. From a hollow another machine gun suddenly chattered viciously. Everything started to crackle as though it were a New Year's Eve party. Far in the distance he could see the fireworks from the flare pistols. Then, abruptly, the noise collapsed like a house of cards. Silence. Only one stray bullet whined through the air. It seemed to fly up into the sky and disappear.

"Smoke another cigarette," the runner said to his men. They stood in a circle around him and the little red points glowed. When one of them drew a puff the outline of his face became visible. A few shots crackled over from the enemy high ground.

"Well, let's go," said the runner and threw his cigarette-butt among the trees. Bent double, the column made its way slowly along the embankment. The runner was in front.

Now they began to meet others going in the opposite direction. Men carrying ammunition boxes wriggled past them. Another runner overtook them. At the aid station black shapes lay on the ground—the dead. Not a sound came from the column. They could see the white glimmer of a carbide lamp in a tent. A smell of carbolic acid and chalk. Some distance away in the forest a battery opened up. In the red glow of the gunfire which flickered in the night sky the runner caught a glimpse of the hill, the high tension pylon, the burnt slope and the shell holes. Continual bursts of machine-gun fire came from the enemy lines. A cloudburst of shells rained down over the rails. At last it broke off, with vindictive satisfaction, as if to say: "We're still here you see."

Now the hill. The runner scrambled up the embankment, ducked and ran up the slope. The mortar shells seemed like falling stones. In a flash he was in the middle of the bombardment and the column too. But he thought only of himself. An inner voice commanded: "Fall flat!" He flung himself to the earth. It ordered again: "Now run for your life!" He began to run. His legs obeyed him instinctively. The hill erupted. Stones, earth and sand roared down upon him, a volcanic rain of red-hot splinters. Suddenly, peace. Not a sound. A single flare swaying in the air.

He stood like a statue, not daring to throw himself down. The slightest movement would cost him his life. The picture of a hundred barrel-mouths aimed at him in the dark made him shiver. His teeth began to chatter. The flare grew brighter.

"Let yourself fall!" whispered the voice of temptation. He could hardly breathe. All that moved were his eyes, searching in the darkness, trying to see the muzzles of the guns pointed at his breast. The beam of the parachute flare flickered. It was like a searchlight. Apart from the pylon, he was the only object standing on the hill. His replacements lay somewhere in the shadows. The searchlight seemed loath to go out. "Now you must let yourself fall!" repeated the tempter. Then the flare died and he leaped forward with a sigh of relief. Like a blind man he ran against the concrete base of the high tension pylon. His hand came in contact with broken glass and his knee burned painfully. Something dark—one of the pylon girders—threatened to fall on him. It did not fall and he plucked up courage to get his breath under cover of the solid concrete.

With the file of men creeping behind him he could not visit the foxhole beneath the pylon. He was a convict who had escaped from jail. Wherever he tried to find cover, a file of prisoners followed him using his escape route. There was but one thing to do—plunge forward again into the darkness.

Going downhill was easier and his own impetus helped him. He was like a ball rolling down a slope, bouncing wildly. The rattle of wooden shoes on an iron bridge accompanied him: mortar shells trying to find him. A branch lashed him in the face. He was already in the undergrowth at the bottom. His feet refused to obey him any more. He relieved himself in the bushes like a man who, once his work is over, remembers his body. He always did this at the same place and he always found it possible. In this respect he was like a dog. Down the slope came the trample of sixty feet—a locomotive of human bodies driven by fear and panic. He had difficulty in stopping them and was very surprised to find there had been no casualties. Together they made their way through the bushy hollow. Tall grass, bushes and thorns tore their uniforms and pierced their flesh. And then they reached the entrance to the trench. Bullets hummed like bees through the branches.

"Wait here until I fetch you," said the runner.

He covered the last stretch to the dugout at the usual speed although no sound of mortar shells could be heard. With relief he kicked aside the iron plate from the entrance, slipped through the crack and got back his breath before he pulled aside the old piece of sacking.

The smell that hit him was like poison gas. Even before he saw the enemy soldier he could already smell him. Disinfectant clung to their uniforms whether they were living or dead.

"A deserter!" said the sergeant major with a gesture as though he had personally fetched him from the enemy trenches.

The Russian sat on the bench in front of the table and the captain was leaning back in his chair on the other side. Each stared at the other as though waiting for him to draw a knife. The Russian had narrow slit eyes and bitten-down finger nails. He was terrified. His short cropped hair stood up on his head.

At last the captain broke the silence. "We're not getting anywhere. He's too upset." He scratched his head and said:

"I'll draw it for him." He paid no attention to the runner. With the help of paper and the pencil he usually chewed he tried to learn from the Russian soldier the position of the enemy trench mortars. He had no success. The man stared at the paper in silence and shrugged his shoulders. The fumes rising from his uniform infected the dugout which already stank badly enough of sweat and filth. The sergeant major raised his hand. "Perhaps he'll understand this," he said bringing it down with a bang on the round cropped skull.

"No," said the captain, "don't hit him." The enemy soldier smiled although he had not understood.

The sergeant major patted his revolver holster. "You have to talk differently to them."

The captain seemed resigned. "He doesn't know anything. We can't do anything about it."

With a smile the Russian took some bits of loose tobacco from his trouser pocket, tore a piece of paper from the drawing and rolled himself a cigarette. He nipped one end of it together so the tobacco would not run out, bent over to the candle and lit it.

"Does that muck taste good?" asked the sergeant major sarcastically.

The soldier gave a broad smile, a childish, peasant-like smile. He looked at the faces of the enemy and found them no different from his own—frightened and distrustful, merely a difference of features. Their desires, like his own, had grown small and unpretentious: a little food, a bit of warmth and not to have to go on suffering. Suddenly his face changed. He looked bewildered as though he must now thank them for the comfort he had not received, for the bang on his head and for the threat of the revolver. He stretched out his arms. It seemed as though he wanted to embrace everything—the key position, the hill, the front line sector, the whole country which lay out there in the darkness. The flame on the candle wobbled. The captain started in his chair. The Russian sat silent on his bench and smiled. But now things had changed. "They're going to attack," suggested the sergeant major. In his mind's eye he already saw figures climbing out of the trenches, a grim game of shadows and abysses, a swaying wall of men after a steely hail of shells.

"My kingdom for an interpreter," said the captain remembering that he had once been a professor.

"We must send him down to battalion headquarters," said the sergeant major.

"That's good," thought the runner. Battalion headquarters. He forgot that he never wanted to make that trip again and that he hated the hill which had to be crossed. But now he would get away from the attack. It was a real stroke of luck. He smiled contentedly, and the foreign soldier smiled back. There was nothing purposeless in this world. He had always been a believer in God and justice. The sergeant major's voice rustled in his ear but he paid no attention. He could already see himself with the prisoner running over the hill, escaping from the danger. The forest would wrap its protecting cloak around him. Then the sergeant major's face floated toward him and a hand patted his shoulder.

"I'll take him back. You're tired."

His voice was gentle and hypnotic.

In a haze the runner saw the captain lolling in his seat and the Russian soldier's smile. "No, I'm not," he pleaded.

"Yes, you are," said the sergeant major.

Suddenly the runner had a vision. He saw the sergeant major leave the dugout with the prisoner. They ran through the pitch black night. The N.C.O. had drawn his revolver and the prisoner obeyed the slightest pressure in his back. A sentry in the trench challenged them. "I'm taking him down to B.H.Q.," replied the sergeant major. Two shadowy figures crossed the saps and were outlined against the undergrowth on the slope. They stumbled up the hill. The sergeant major made the prisoner run on ahead. Farther, farther. They ran through mud, shell holes and sand. They grew smaller . . .

"I've brought reinforcements from the battalion," the runner heard himself say, but the sergeant major had already left the dugout with the prisoner.

It was dark, as usual, in the hole under the concrete foundation. The corporal squatted between his two comrades with his legs drawn up under his chin. They lay in mouldy blankets on the damp earth. Their breath wheezed. The cold night wind blew through the entrance. The N.C.O. was on watch and because he was tired he lit a pipe. At the moment it was peaceful on the hill. No dull thuds of mortar shells, no hammering of artillery. He listened, but no sound of shelling disturbed the night. The time passed slowly on his watch and the unusual silence irritated him. The air suddenly seemed to have become charged with electricity.

He stood up and stumbled over his two sleeping comrades to the entrance. Slowly he hoisted himself out of the hole. A light breeze ruffled his hair. Above him towered the pylon. A piece of steel girder which a shell had ripped off lay like a black shadow in front of him. The wind carried over a rumble from the enemy positions. It sounded as though a huge truck were unsuccessfully trying to make its way up a hill. Far away to the left he could see noiseless strands of tracer bullets in the darkness. Sparks fell into the water like rain and were extinguished. Some moments later he could hear the sound of the firing.

The corporal felt for his flare pistol. There was dew on the leather holster. The trigger clicked back. He stretched out his arm and fired. There was a dull report. The rocket hissed away and a few seconds later, above the positions, lit up like a falling star. The comet flew toward the enemy trenches. Then the parachute opened and in the magnesium light he realized he had not aimed high enough. Instead of swaying over the hill the flare wobbled over the low ground. In front of him lay the deserted positions. No movement. No sign of life. A graveyard in the moonlight. Tree clumps looming like gravestones. A puddle of water like a pond without water lilies. The labyrinth of trenches. The bushes like a cemetery wall. The flare sank lower and gradually smoldered away on the ground. The corporal laid his submachine gun on the parapet and waited. He removed the safety catch. The pylon hummed. His wrist watch ticked. Suddenly out of the darkness came the sound of shuffling feet. He put his gun up to his shoulder immediately.

At that moment a searchlight from the artillery positions swept the hill and he could see a figure, a soldier in enemy uniform making his way towards him.

Before the light went out the corporal had his finger on the trigger. *"Nicht schiessen, Kamerad,"* came a scream. "Don't shoot!"

Quick as lightning the corporal raised up the barrel. The Russian soldier before him slumped to the ground. An unbearable silence. The sweat poured down the N.C.O.'s forehead and his hands were trembling. Suddenly the voice of the sergeant major asked out of the darkness, "Is he dead?"

The sergeant major climbed out of the shell hole and came over to the man on watch who was tempted to level his gun again.

"Who was that?" he asked.

"Only a prisoner."

"A pretty good shield, eh?"

The sergeant major was now standing close to the corporal and could see the automatic weapon. "Don't worry about it," he said after an oppressive silence, but he prudently took a step to one side. "Good night," he called in

47

a shaky voice, ran around the base of the pylon and disappeared into the darkness.

The corporal fetched a spade to cover the Russian's corpse with earth. The pylon hummed in the wind. The tractor noises behind the enemy trenches had stopped. In the hole beneath the ground the corporal lay down and chewed his finger nails in despair.

Chapter Three

THE STABLE DOOR closed behind Captain Sostschenko. He
stood there staring into the night. His eyes had to get ac-
customed to the darkness. They were still blinded by the
light and he tried to forget Sonja who was lying there in
the stable. There was no sign of his Siberian shock battalion which had been alerted along the light rail track.
Somewhere, mercifully hidden by the night, there was a
hill which he had to storm with them, presumably just as
the sun rose or in the early dawn. Sonja in the stable was a
memory to which one said farewell, as though by command. To take his mind off Sonja he thought of the general's broad epaulettes. It had been at an officers' confer-
ence in Nevorosk. A Corps officer had ticked off the units
for the approaching attack: The Red Star Regiment, the
Ufa Armoured Truck Unit, Kolkhoz Dynamo, Rocket Detachment Lenin, the Moscow, Marx and Robot Mortar
Regiments.

"*Are you in charge of the Siberians?*"

"*Yes, Comrade General.*"

"*Do you know the details of the attack?*"

"*Yes, Comrade General.*"

"*The tanks will only go as far as the German barbed wire. There the marsh begins. If you and your men stay behind the tanks the attack will fail. Perhaps that would be the end. Tell that to your men and don't forget to give the signal for the stretcher bearers after the break-through.*"

"*Yes, Comrade General.*"

Sostschenko remembered every word. Only as far as the barbed wire. There the marsh begins. Here was the weak point of the plan. Sostschenko's battalion was to be sacrificed on the cornerstone of the enemy front. They were to die for a diversionary maneuver. A sacrifice for a larger plan.

At that moment it broke loose. A tongue of fire shot into the sky. Its light sprang from one horizon to the other. The captain stood in the center of a fiery circle. The earth opened and spat out burning lava. A deafening roll of thunder as the artillery regiment sent out its salvos. The shells roared like a mountain torrent. For the first time he spotted the barrels of the big guns behind the camouflage nets. The barrels fell, reached their lowest point, were raised again already reloaded by unseen hands. Metal breeches clicked.

In the light of the gun flashes Sostschenko saw the gunners at work, deliberate, as if they were performing some sacrificial rite. Eyes intoxicated by the flocks of fiery birds, ears deafened by the uproar, nerves taut, he shouted. He recognized the crouching figures on the light rail track as his Siberians. "Forward!" came the jubilant command from an inner voice. For one moment he hesitated and then the voice propelled him into action.

The fiery carnival had begun.

The captain looked into the staring eyes of the runner and screamed. They both opened their mouths and then the blast flung them into the dugout. The red sky, the darkness, the face of the other man, everything revolved at a crazy speed like figures on a roulette wheel round an invisible axis. Lungs were bursting for lack of breath. Both of them were hurled like bundles of old rags against the wall. This was the end or the beginning.

The runner dreamed: someone had brought a flask into the dugout and placed it on the table. He recognized the label but could not read the writing. Either the label or the bottle was standing upside down. He felt a need to empty his bladder. As he prepared to do so he felt a burning pain in his right hand. I'm bleeding to death, he thought. He next found himself in a cathedral. A hundred voices were singing a hymn and the song echoed against the stained glass windows. In the center of the nave hung a golden crucifix. That was the peace he had always sought. He stretched out his hand and then woke up. Something cold ran down his back and made him shiver. He returned to consciousness and to ruthless clarity. A terrible fear took hold of him. Blood had congealed between his fingers. It was oozing out of his body into the darkness. Suddenly he understood what was happening: mortar shells flying over, one after the other, along assigned paths, falling exactly on the front line. One wave of steel boring into the ground while another sped through the air and a third was already being fired out of the barrels. An attack by a regiment, a division, or a whole army, and the center of this attack lay in front of his own trench.

The earth swayed beneath the runner's feet and the barrage crept closer. It fell first on the trenches, then on the communication sap and the dugout, moving upwards onto the hill, across the pylon and then down the other side into the woods, on to the heavy batteries. It had been inevitable and this was the end.

A blast of air swept through the dugout. The runner pressed himself to the ground. He must wait until the barrage lifted or the dugout buried him. Two layers of logs above his head, logs a foot in diameter covered with two feet of earth. Either they would stand up or they would not. *Lieber Gott im Himmel!*

Earth fell from the roof. A direct hit. Splintering wood. The dugout rocked. The sheet iron of the door was like a leaf in the wind. The space under the reinforced roof seemed about to burst. But the runner was alive. The two layers of logs had held fast. They will not stand up to the next hit, thought the runner. But there won't be another one. He was an old soldier: the gunners would not hit the same place twice. The barrage shifted slowly and was now well behind the dugout.

He struck a match and looked at his hand. There was a large cut inside his thumb—a superficial wound, that was all. He was ashamed of his fear. The captain was groaning at his side. The match went out and he called out in the darkness: "*Herr Hauptmann?*" The air smelt of powder. Mortar shells were exploding outside on top of the log roof. There was a taste of bitter almonds on his tongue.

"Have you got a cigarette?" asked the captain.

"Yes." He stretched out his bloodstained hand in the dark and stuck it in a pot of jam. He felt sick and quickly withdrew his hand.

Suddenly he heard the captain's voice saying: "What's going on?"

"A saturation barrage."

His voice sounded pathetic and rather reproachful. Just outside the dugout a jet of flame ran along the trench.

"I think I fainted," said the captain. Shrapnel and stones thudded against the iron of the entrance door. "I'm wounded," retorted the runner. At that he stood up and felt along the wall, which continued to tremble like a machine casing. The earth was cold and damp. The fire was now concentrated on the pocket below the hill. He could hear this from the hollow explosions. The heavy mortars were plastering the swamp. Light artillery shells hammered continuously onto the roof of the dugout.

"Can't you get some light going?" The captain's voice sounded peevish. "Call up the company," he commanded.

The runner groped for the field telephone; he fumbled about on the ground. The table had disappeared and the floor was covered with wooden splinters. At last he got hold of the bakelite box. The receiver had fallen out. He turned on the switch and listened but not a sound could be heard in the headphones. "The connection's broken, sir." While waiting for a reply he felt along the wire and after about a yard came to the place where it had snapped.

"Try to get us some light," said the captain wearily.

"I can't find the lamp."

"Good God!" said the captain. "You should be able to find a candle somewhere!"

Time went by and the thunder outside went on with undiminished severity. The din ebbed and flowed. The captain had found a tallow candle. When the flame caught, it hardly cast a shadow. On the roof the woven branches were shifting and earth trickled down into the dugout. The captain was squatting on the ground. "What's wrong with your hand?" he asked.

"It's ripped open. A piece of shrapnel. It's burning like fire."

"I can't let you go on that account."

The runner nodded. "I know," he said. He tried to smile. It was the only thing to do in the circumstances but all he could summon was a pathetic grimace. A handful of stones rattled through the entrance. He raised his hands to his eyes.

"Direct hit." said the captain.

Outside it seemed as though freight cars were rolling into each other. Then a breathing space, a short terrifying silence, and out of the silence a piercing shriek. It came from the trenches in front, broke on the dugout entrance and died away—the death shriek of a man who rears up once again before the blood gushes from his mouth. The runner stared into the candle flame as though he had not heard it. The captain raised his hand in the air in a defensive gesture. Then both of them stared at the roof where the logs were gradually being smashed to pieces by the mortar shells. Time was like a river. The minutes passed and each of them seemed an eternity. Sometimes, for a change, there was a hail of rockets. Heavy calibre shells struck intermittently like gongs. A grey dawn began to trickle through the entrance. It was pale and lifeless, like a shroud to cover a dead man.

Suddenly a shadow loomed on the steps and a figure stumbled in. The runner noticed a bloody arm stump hanging from the torn mud-stained uniform. The stump moved, as though the missing lower limb were still feeling for support.

A voice groaned: *"Kamaraden. . . ."*

The wounded man stumbled and the runner caught him. The other man's blood ran over his hand. He reached for a strap and put a tourniquet on the stump. The sweat poured down his face. The wounded man looked at him as though he were working on a piece of wood. While he rolled the bandage round the hanging strips of flesh, he shook with horror.

The wounded man giggled. "If I ever get out of here," he said, "I'll be all set." And he ended with a satisfied: "For good." The runner looked at the bandage which was turning red and fell silent.

"I'm going to have a try," said the wounded man grimly

and cast a look of hatred at the entrance which was wreathed in a cloud of powder smoke. "I must try and get over the hill," he said obstinately.

"Sit down," said the runner pointing to a wire cot in the corner.

"No one has a right to keep me here."

"Of course not."

"Then I can go now?"

"Yes."

"Well, then. . . ." The wounded man bit his lip, stumbled and fell to the floor. "It'll be too late for me when they attack," he said wearily. In pain and despair he began to sob. There was blood on his jacket, blood on his face, blood everywhere except *in* his lips.

"When the attack's over," said the captain, "we'll get you back." His voice was unsteady.

The wounded man shook his head: "So you don't know?"

"What?"

"There's no company left."

The runner turned and stared at the captain. Mortar shells continued to thud on the roof of the dugout. A large lump of earth fell off the wall and crumbled on the floor.

"How does it look?" asked the captain.

"Bad." The wounded man tried to raise himself but he was too weak. The runner put a pack under his head. "Flame thrower. . . . direct hit. The men were burned up." He found it difficult to breathe. "Nothing left round my machine gun but lumps of flesh. Matz—killed outright.

Shrapnel in the head." The pain made him writhe. "Hager's still alive but they can't bandage him. His guts are hanging out."

The runner ducked at an explosion just outside the dugout. When he looked at the wounded man's face again it was weeping silently.

"All I could see of Fadinger was his hand." The wounded man closed his eyes. "It was lying in the trench when I ran back. I recognized it by the ring. We both wore the same ring. At first I thought it was my own hand but I wear mine on the left." He raised his good hand as if to prove it.

"That's it!" he sobbed. Suddenly he stretched out his hand to the runner. "Take it off, man. I can't stand to look at it any more."

The runner took the ring off and it cost him more self-control than the bandaging of the man's arm stump had done. He tried to stuff it into the man's pocket.

"No, throw it away!" he screamed.

With a frightened gesture the runner threw the ring out of the door. He meant to throw it out of the shaft and into the trenches but he aimed too high. The ring hit the roof just before the steps and rolled down again.

The runner and the captain exchanged glances. Neither of them felt like getting up and trying again. They did not move.

"When I was hit I just ran away," said the wounded man. "Should I have done anything else?"

There was no reply.

"Should I have done anything else?"

"No!" screamed the captain. "No!" He got control of himself immediately. "I'm sorry!"

"What about the sergeant?" asked the runner.

The wounded man tried to smile.

"He's lying behind the machine gun and swearing. You know how he is. A shell hit the belt box."

"Any ammunition in it?"

"There had been," said the wounded man.

The runner stood up. Bending down he felt in the corner of the dugout for a box of machine-gun belts. He closed the lid, grabbed the handles and made his way almost ceremoniously to the steps. When he caught sight of the ring lying there he hesitated for a moment. "Let it stay there," cried the wounded man.

The runner turned around and saw that the man was still lying with his back to the exit. When the ring had fallen back into the dugout he did not think the wounded soldier had noticed it.

"Maybe it's a sign," said the wounded man. "The ring will stay here and I'll stay too."

The runner turned and got ready to jump. Not even noticing the weight of the box, he was out of the dugout in one bound and rushing along the communication trench. The six-foot trench had been turned into a shallow furrow. In places it had been flattened out and in others the parapet had been blown away. He was running in a small riverbed whose banks bubbled with a mixture of smoke and shrapnel splinters. Stones rained down on him and the earth was thrown up in sprays. There was no point in falling flat. There was only one alternative—to get through as quickly as possible. The shells seemed to be chasing him and at every moment he thought that his back would be blown to pieces. The ammunition box grew heavier. Dirt and sweat poured down his face. He must go on. A white bank of mist hung over the front line and he made for it. The sergeant must be lying somewhere out there in the dampness. He crossed through the tattered edge of mist near the wreck of a shot-up tank. Here the fire was weaker. Panting, he dodged around the tank treads which hung over into the trench—and was suddenly staring into the end of a revolver.

"Have you gone crazy?" the runner screamed at the sentry.

The man lowered his weapon in fright. He stared after the runner as though he had just seen a ghost which had vanished again into the white broth. The runner hurried on with his box. Stumbled over something soft. Fell into something sticky and picked himself up full of disgust. On again. He came to the front line. He could tell by the slippery duck boards over which he now slid along.

An abandoned sentry post with only the rifle leaning against the parapet. He noticed now for the first time that there was no mortar fire here. Damp clumps of brush hung lopsided over the position. Yawning bomb craters. White mist. Collapsed trench walls. Parapets blown in. Up ahead of him a heavy shell fell in the barbed-wire entanglement. Not far away he could see empty mine boxes in the fog.

He must soon reach the machine-gun post. A dark patch suddenly loomed ahead of him.

He fell exhausted at the sergeant's feet. He recognized him only by his eyes. Everything else, the steel helmet on the back of his head, the protruding hair, the forehead, cheeks, throat—his whole body—were covered with muck.

"You of all people," he said laconically as he recognized the runner.

"It's me all right," was the reply as he dragged the ammunition box onto the parapet.

"I was just about to smash the firing pin."

They lifted up the tripod and snapped the catch on the barrel.

"How long ago did you stop shooting?"

"A couple of minutes," said the sergeant putting in the new belt.

"Who's that?" asked the runner pointing to a dead man on the parapet. He wanted to drag him down.

"Leave him there," said the sergeant. "He's not a pretty sight from the front."

"Did he get it in the stomach?"

"Something like that. It was only a shrapnel splinter."

A shell tore a rift in the fog ahead of them.

"Over there!" The sergeant pulled the gun to his shoulder. The runner looked into the rift. He could see nothing but the mist billowing over the shell holes beyond. Between the wire and their own trenches lay the marsh. The fog above them had turned into a fine drizzle. Transparent as glass. The rift closed again, slowly whirling together.

Shells rattled overhead in the air. Behind them, falling ever further away, in their blind rage they bored into the swamp in front of the hill.

Captain Sostschenko crossed a damp meadow. A hollow in the ground lay ahead of him. He ordered the men to wait there below. His own batteries now lay behind them. Their fire had a deeper ring. The bombardment raged at furious tempo and the forest in the west looked like a burning city. He kept on thinking that the attack must succeed and clutched this hope like an inexperienced child. Later, the general had said, the battalion would remain in reserve on the high ground. This word too he weighed in the balance: later. A word can often be an encouragement whether one believes it or not.

On the German side, minefields were being blown in the air, the barbed wire was cut, the dugouts were smashed. Nevertheless Sostschenko was not at ease. His instinct refused to be silenced. He pushed his way through the Red Army soldiers, heard them talking in undertones and felt their warm breath in the night air. Someone accidentally brushed his arm but he remained alone. Alone with his conscience, his critical intelligence and his oppressive memories. He stared vacantly into space. The cold began to numb his limbs. He felt an uncomfortable pressure on his temples and a trace of fever. He stamped mechanically on the ground to get his feet warm. The hand of his watch seemed to crawl around the dial.

As dawn broke he breathed a sigh of relief. His word of

command set a file of three hundred men in motion. They disappeared into the communication trench, into a maze of crumbling corridors and bays full of excrement and filth. In the dugouts lay unserviceable weapons and empty ammunition boxes. The infantry company had already abandoned its positions. A corpse hung over the parapet. A blood-stained bandage lay in a pile of sand.

Sostschenko ran, stooping, through the sections and again looked at his watch. Another twenty minutes. In another twenty minutes three hundred Siberians would climb out of the trenches and attack. In thirty minutes they would know the result. The nearer zero hour approached, the more unreal it was. In the morning grey he realized that in half an hour his future would be decided. It was like a dream. When I wake up, he thought, it will all be over. He hoisted himself up on the parapet and, glued to the earth, examined the country ahead. In the faint light he could make out the hill: a bare, lifeless thing under a hail of iron, half lost in smoke. Mortar shells were now plastering the high ground, raising columns of sand. Clouds of smoke trailed through the shell holes. The skeleton of the high tension pylon was still standing. Despite the explosions a sinister silence seemed to reign over this hill.

Suddenly a faint humming. Sostschenko turned round. The noise increased. A roar of engines and a rattle of tracks. The tanks. Muddy steel turrets floated out of the mist and broke from the undergrowth. The heads of the commanding officers stuck out of the turrets. The earth trembled. The monsters fanned out and came to rest just short of the occupied trenches. Farther back in the grey light they could still see the flashes from their own artillery.

Sostschenko raised his arm. Nine minutes to go.

Lieutenant Trupikow hurried along the communication trench.

"Battalion ready for action, Captain." His face was like a mask.

"Good!" replied Sostschenko. He was surprised at the indifference in his own voice. He saw that Trupikow was checking his submachine gun, tightening the straps of his steel helmet round his chin and arranging the hand grenades at his belt. Like movements behind a pane of glass. Stiff as a marionette. He himself had also become a puppet, imprisoned in a body which could only react clumsily. He turned over on his back and raised his arm so he could keep his eye on the tanks and the dial of his watch. Another four minutes.

"Get ready!"

Trupikow passed on the order and his cry was drowned by the noise of engines. Three minutes.

A cold shudder ran through his body. At his side green steel helmets bobbed up and eyes were focused on him. Two minutes.

The second hand began to scuttle like a little animal. A hundred seconds, eighty seconds, sixty. . . .

The tanks advanced, the tracks tightened. In formation they crawled over the trench, swayed in the air, slumped on the parapet and flattened out the trench. A steel wall careened past Sostschenko. He stood up and rushed forward. Behind him came a host of men. Caterpillar tracks ploughed up the earth, sprinkling his face with mud.

He roared like an angry bull: "Hurrah, hurrah . . . hurrah!"

It seemed that a pack of angry dogs was being driven towards them. The cries hung and echoed in the moist air. The sergeant swung the barrel of his machine gun. He could not see the target. Nothing but the thin lines of barbed wire. They hung like ghostly spider webs in the white mist.

"I am going crazy," whispered the runner. Suddenly a machine gun spat away to the left and at the same moment, ahead of them, a black mass appeared, cutting through the mist. The black colossus moved towards them like a ship. And again the wild yelling behind the protective wall of the tank.

The sergeant did not move.

"Let's get out of here!" screamed the runner raising himself on his hands in an attempt to leave.

"Stay where you are!" The sergeant hit him on the back. The runner obeyed. "It won't get farther than the wire. They've never come beyond the marsh."

"We're the last. We can't hold out." The runner in his excitement ran his hand over the machine-gun belt as though he wanted to stroke it.

"Are you scared?"

"Yes."

"So am I," said the sergeant calmly.

"Fire!"

The tank reached the wire in front of the marsh and came to a halt.

"Now!" whispered the sergeant. He aimed carefully. Rifle fire still came from their left and the other machine gun was still firing. Figures suddenly appeared from behind the tank, stuck close to the tank walls and advanced beyond it.

"Fire!" gasped the runner.

"Hand grenades!" ordered the sergeant.

With flying fingers the runner unscrewed the safety caps. Ahead, the brown figures, with angular movements, had entered the barbed wire. They cleared themselves a passage with the butts of their tommy-guns. The lid of the tank turret opened and a leather helmet appeared. The sergeant pulled the machine-gun lever to single shot and aimed at this helmet. A loud report. The helmet slipped back into the turret. The sergeant changed over to automatic fire, lowered the barrel and fired a burst into the figures on the barbed wire. They came to a stop and looked up. One of them raised his arms, others began to reel like drunken men. The remainder flung themselves to the ground. It had lasted only a couple of seconds. The men had been swept away. Here and there one of them moved on the ground and the sergeant aimed at these quivering movements.

Mud flew up from the wire. From behind a small hillock an arm was raised and a hand grenade swept through the air. It burst in front of them in the marsh. There was a muffled explosion and filthy water spurted over their heads.

The runner grasped the pile of grenades on the parapet. He stuck a cord between his fingers and was about to pull it out. Before he could stand up the sergeant hit him on the arm and the runner slipped back into his hole. A hand emerged from the tank turret into which the helmet had disappeared, grasped the lid and closed it. From the cover behind the tank tracks, gun flashes appeared, firing at them. A spray from a tommy-gun ploughed up the earth just in front of them.

"Damn, they've spotted us!" said the sergeant dropping the gun and ducking. "You can throw them now!" he said excitedly. "Throw them!"

Automatically the runner pulled the cord and flung the hand grenade out of the hole.

"Go on, go on!"

The runner took one after the other, ripped the cords, did not wait for the explosions, flung them away.

"That's enough!" said the sergeant. Two hand grenades still lay there in front of them. He carefully raised his head over the parapet. He saw the barrel on the tank being lowered exactly in the direction of their hole.

"Take cover!" he roared.

But the shell had already left the barrel. It whizzed sharply over their heads, leaving behind it a trail of hot air. It exploded beyond them.

"Get out of here!"

66

The sergeant tore the belt out of the machine gun, pulled it down and jumped back into the trench.

"To the left!" he shouted.

The runner slammed down the lid of the ammunition box and seized the handles. The hinge fell back and the contents of the box clattered into the trench.

"Leave it there!" The sergeant was already running along the trench carrying the machine gun like a child in his arms. The runner grabbed both hand grenades and rushed after him.

The N.C.O. came to a stop. In front of him lay one of the replacements. His eyes were closed and he seemed to be asleep. A thin red trickle ran from his mouth like a cord of silk. His fingers were still clutching his gun.

"Take it!" said the sergeant.

The runner bent down, but the dead man's fingers would not release the weapon and he had to stamp on his arm.

"Take the ammunition too."

He laid the dead man on his side, took the ammunition from the canvas case at his side. Behind them a flare went up from the position they had just left.

"They're already in the trench." The sergeant hurried on.

"No!" said the runner. He stood up and looked at the sergeant major. "I'm giving myself up!"

The sergeant looked at him sardonically. "Idiot! So you're depending on your pass are you?"

"I couldn't care less!"

The sergeant dropped his gun and, before the runner

knew what had happened, slapped him hard on both cheeks.

"That's by way of goodbye," said the N.C.O. with obvious satisfaction.

He picked up the machine gun, turned around and ran off. The runner saw him disappear. Hand grenades burst behind him. He began to run, too. After a short time they came to a halt.

They heard the sound of weeping coming from a hole in the parapet. The sergeant bent down and pulled the soldier out by his boots. It was another of the replacements. The runner recognized him by his protruding teeth. His moist eyes were dark ringed and he looked almost exactly as he had looked that night in the light of the parachute flare.

"Are you wounded?"

The question was superfluous. In his jacket near the hip, was a hole as big as a fist. A ball of cotton wool fell out.

"Take me with you . . ."

Without a word the sergeant dropped his machine gun, lifted the soldier up and slung him over his shoulder. They went on running. The wounded man stopped weeping. Now he groaned only when the sergeant stumbled.

The hammering of the machine guns ahead of them grew louder.

The sergeant began to shout. It was a monotonous cry as though he were steering a boat in the fog. "Don't shoot! Don't shoot!" at regular short intervals.

"Who goes there?" they suddenly heard from behind a bend.

"Give the password," the sergeant said to the runner. "Dresden!"

"All right. You can advance."

The soldier stood behind a canvas-covered barrier which blocked off the trench. Two of his mates were leaning against a Russian machine gun which stood on the roof.

"A mighty fortress is our God," said the sergeant as he helped lift the wounded man over the obstacle.

"Are they already in the trenches?"

"We're the last of ours," said the sergeant as he entered the "hedgehog." He pointed to the rear where the machine gun they had recently heard had begun to bark.

"What's going on?"

"They're trying a frontal attack under cover of the fog but they haven't succeeded. They've got stuck in the marsh and we're mowing them down."

"Good!" said the sergeant. "And now I'll take over command." He saw the runner climb over the barrier and the canvas wobble slightly. He gave a start. A pile of lifeless figures slipped down. The men had piled corpses on top of each other to make a breastwork.

"*Mein Gott!*" stammered the runner.

"Don't let it get you down," said the sergeant. "The Good Lord must be pleased, otherwise he wouldn't have allowed it." He carefully rolled himself a cigarette. "The emphasis is on the *good*," he said sarcastically.

The runner was silent.

"You go and take a look at the wounded, but don't tell them that we're surrounded and that we can't get them back."

The runner made off into the sap.

"Say yes, sir," the sergeant called after him. He received no reply. The runner had disappeared into the mist. Suddenly the sergeant felt sorry for him.

Chapter Four

FROM THE SHELTER of the tank Sostschenko fired his tommy gun at the German machine gun half hidden in the mist. The hand grenade bursts had given away the position. Then there was a rattle of shrapnel against the iron plates of the tank and he had to fling himself to the ground..

He noticed that the first shot from the tank gun was too high. The second was a direct hit on the machine-gun nest. The tank commander had slumped down into the turret with a wound in the head. To Sostschenko it was like a bad dream. Ten or twelve of his Siberian troops were hanging with broken limbs in the barbed wire. In front of him the fog, at his side the tank. As though from afar he heard the throb of the engine. He was surrounded by his Red Army soldiers but as always he was alone. Lieutenant Trupikow was crouching in a hollow waiting for his example. He had lost all contact with reality.

Soloviev had stood near him and blinked his eyes as always. He had wanted to say something. One could still see this by his eyes and mouth. His whole face had shown it. But then he had said nothing, had merely looked with startled eyes as though he had stepped barefoot on a glass splinter. Not excessively upset. No sign of fear. An unpleasant surprise which in actual fact was not too bad. This was how he had greeted death. Sostschenko did not know where he had been hit. Soloviev sat down, not the way a man usually sits down but not like a wounded man either. Slightly surprised but content. And with that, he was already dead.

Sostschenko had seen all this with incredulous amazement. How could a man die unprepared like that, not even able to complete a thought or able to utter the word that was already forming on his lips. Where was the conclusion, the culmination? What had Soloviev wanted to ask him? He had seen other men die, strangers, as alien as the Red Army soldiers who now stood round him waiting for something. What were they waiting for?

It was time to get up and climb through the strands of wire. Into the blanket of fog. Barbed wire. A fine drizzle of rain . . . exactly as it had been one day so long ago . . .

Murmansk. The harbor. The pier wall with iron stakes and barbed wire. A soldier in the fog. The barrel of his rifle gleaming with bright drops of water. He himself, a youngster soaked to the skin and freezing. But he was a soldier and did not dare abandon his post. On the other side were the enemy in the white mist. A cold wind blew in from the sea. In the distance, the muffled sound of a foghorn. Pacing up and down the barbed wire. A game for a dreamy youngster in a sailor suit, who got soaked through and returned home with a touch of fever. Mamma un-

dressed him and asked no questions. She held his small hot hand and looked at him. The little boy did not want to be alone any longer. He pressed his mother's hand to his lips. He put his arms around her, and she waited until he fell asleep. . . .

Sostschenko climbed over the last wire. The Siberian troops were at his side. His boots sank in the marsh. He stuck in the slime and advanced only with difficulty. Brown puddles. Green patches of moss the shells had spared . . .

The cemetery in Murmansk. Brown puddles of water. His boots sank into the clay. Mamma's black coffin covered with a moss-green blanket. Four men with bored faces. The bearded patriarch. Strangers who tried to comfort him. Mamma, dear Mamma, take me with you. Don't leave me alone. . . . His mother didn't hear him any more. All that was left: a little mound of up-turned earth. . . .

Up-turned earth. Sostschenko saw the shell holes and the shot-up machine-gun nest. He seemed to see it all through glass. He climbed into the trench and stood on a duck board. In front of him lay an ammunition box with a sprung lid. The belts were slopping out of it. . . .

On the wet station platform. At his feet lay his suitcase with a sprung lid. Underwear slopped out of it. Many strangers staring at him as he stood there by the suitcase. Someone laughed. Nobody helped him put the things back inside. The train whistled. The travelers sprang to life. He tried to grab his things. Someone bumped him. The crowd surged forward. No one paid any attention. The youngster in the shabby sailor suit again tried to bend down to his suitcase. It was kicked away. Feet trampled on his linen. A dirty heel ground into his mother's picture. . . .

Sostschenko hurried along the trench and climbed over dead German soldiers. He was followed by Lieutenant Trupikow. They came to a small sap which led to the high ground. Sostschenko emptied a magazine of his submachine gun into the sap. Ahead of him lay a wrecked tank hanging perilously over the trench. The trench made a bend around it. On the ground crouched a figure with its hands above its head. Sostschenko aimed but his fingers were numb. Let Lieutenant Trupikow do it. Trupikow's revolver spat. The German soldier fell with his hands still above his head. Trupikow handed Sostschenko the flare pistol. A lilac flare rose in the sky. A falling star fell to earth . . .

But as the falling star fell through the leaves of the trees and sank to earth in the forest it was no longer a star but a white robe with golden wings. The child took the robe and was turned into an angel. He no longer felt the cold and now he was no longer alone. He winged his way to join the other angels in heaven. The Good Lord had called him as he calls all the pure in heart. Take care then that your heart too remains pure. . . . Mamma blew out the lamp and kissed him in the dark on the cheek . . .

The trench forked. A broad sap led to the rear and a communication trench to the right hardly wide enough to wriggle through. From ahead came the rattle of an enemy machine gun. Sostschenko turned off to the right. He must get around to the rear of the enemy machine gun. That was his duty. Trupikow went along the sap and Sostschenko followed the windings of the narrow trench between high damp earthen walls . . .

The high bare walls in the orphanage cellar. The corridor had many turns and the water dripped from the whitewashed walls. He had to run alone through dark corridors. His heart beat furiously and he was breathless. Shadows stretched out their hands to clutch him but he had to go on. The matron insisted upon it. Blows and punishments make men of children. Fear of pain. Fear is the mother of action. Fear maintains order. Endless fear. The youngster ran with bare feet over the cold flagstones. Above him was the dormitory with three hundred children. Three hundred shivering little bodies on straw pallets. Three hundred children hungry for love. The youngster had to run because he had been ordered to. . . .

The communication trench had fallen in. Shells had crumbled the walls. Sostschenko climbed out of it. The sweat made his uniform stick to his body. He stood there panting in the mist on the ploughed up earth. Shell holes all around. Ahead in the fog the enemy machine gun clattered. He was now directly to the rear of the gunner. Had there been no mist he could have fired at him. The veil of mist flattened out and he could see the labyrinth of trenches. All along the trench behind him were green helmets—little round targets on a firing range. . . .

The round targets were moving past on a wire, green targets with a black circle in the middle. A barrel organ whined. . . . Sostschenko, the cadet, shot at the targets with

*an air rifle. Beside him stood a black haired girl with bright
eyes and a half-open mouth. Cadet Sostschenko did not
hit the target because he was excited. The girl Sonja smiled.
He blushed. His uniform stuck to his skin. The girl pulled
him away. Her hand was cool and it was the hand of a
woman. . . .*

Men were approaching the spot where Sostschenko had
climbed into the trench. As they came out of the mist one
could see they were in line. Red soldiers in twos carrying
logs. They staggered under the load. They dropped the
logs, rolled them into the soft morass and, in twos, disappeared back into the mist. A noiseless game. An orderly
coming and going, making a crossing for the tanks. Now
the engineer company's orders had been carried out. The
giants rolled forward. The first tank ripped up the damp
earth and skidded on the water-splashed wood. The others
followed nose to tail. They bit into the logs and crawled
slowly forward. Soon the leading tank had reached the
trench and once more had firm ground beneath its tracks.
The second followed suit but the third one began to wobble. Its tracks splayed the logs, throwing some of them six
feet into the air. Sostschenko heard the splintering of wood.
The tracks spun wildly in the void. Only for a few seconds,
and then the monster began to sink. The gun barrel listed
and the tracks went on spinning wildly trying to get a
purchase. The tank was digging its own grave and sinking
deeper and deeper into the slime. Now only the mud-
stained turret was visible. The black giant sank in a muddy
whirlpool. The exhaust pipes spat out a last fountain of

mud. The tank following close behind skidded into the hole, nor could the next one avoid it. The gong beats of colliding steel plates sounded in Sostschenko's ears. Three tanks disappeared into the marsh. Tatters of mist wafted by. A pale, ghostlike picture. All that remained were two black monsters lurching nervously among the labyrinth of trenches towards the high ground. . . .

Two lonely people. The girl Sonja who was now a woman; Cadet Sostschenko who was now a captain. Not even the war could part them. Was she still lying in the stable, in the hay, among the little steaming horses?

Out of the mist something pounced on him. A hot stab tore through his thigh. He tumbled backwards with cramped fingers and drawn features. Why didn't he hear the machine gun any more? A shadow sprang towards him. Hard bony fingers clutched his throat. His eyes wide with fear, he saw a grotesque mask above him. He could feel the man's warm breath on his face. Which was the greater —the burning pain in his thigh, or his fear? He did not know. . . .

The German soldier noticed that his enemy was no longer moving. He stood up. His bayonet was red with blood. He cleaned it in the earth and put it back in the scabbard. The match box he had been about to open lay in the trench. He stared in bewilderment at the figure lying there in a heap. An officer. He was still breathing. Blood was trickling from his wound. A red enamel star gleamed on his breast. His steel helmet was pushed to the back of his head. Hair wet with sweat, fingers spread out. Under his right arm was a tommy-gun. The soldier kicked it aside. This was essential, as he knew from experience.

The soldier leaned against the parapet and his knees shook. Each of the enemy officer's movements hurt him. He felt the pain in the other man's thigh and he could have screamed. Without taking his eyes off the wounded man's face he reached for his gun. Just then the Russian slowly opened his eyes and the soldier knew that he would not shoot. The other man's eyes watched in amazement. They did not seem to understand.

The soldier leaned his gun against the parapet, knelt down and stroked the wounded man's hand. In the mist the machine gun was still firing wildly. The soldier slid one arm under the Russian's head, grasped him around the knees with the other, and lifted him. Stumbling as he went, he carried his burden along the trench to the machine-gun post.

Chapter Five

THE HUTS along the road were burning. Wooden shingles and thatched roofs were a mass of flames. The artillery colonel's house—the house built in French style—was burning at the end of the village of Podrowa. Flames were even licking the woodwork of the village pump. The metal battalion flag creaked in the hot wind. Only the major's hut still stood undamaged, like a black box in the smoke.

The major telephoned: "When I tell you Podrowa is in flames. When I tell you that before long our telephone communications will be broken off. When for half an hour the Russian artillery has been bombarding this hole and their planes have been throwing incendiaries at us without a break—then you can be damned sure this isn't a local skirmish but that the Russians have gone over to the attack."

"My dear Schnitzer," replied the voice at the other end of the line, "according to all our intelligence reports, we here at the division know that this is absolutely out of the question. We're being subjected to a local, concentrated attack on the key position and once more it is a question of that miserable hill. The general is of the opinion that

79

your company will get the upper hand. He has said for you to keep in close touch with me."

"I've been keeping in close touch with you for an hour," said the major rather louder than was necessary, although the crackle of fire could plainly be heard through the broken windowpanes and he was obliged to shout.

The man at the other end of the wire did not seem to notice the raised voice. "Of course," he replied, "but you're not telling me anything new. Strong enemy fire on the key position and the hill. The barrage has shifted slowly toward the rear and reached the Podrowa line half an hour ago. I received the same information from the infantry, the light and heavy artillery, the observers in your sector and from the antiaircraft company. All I want to know from you is: what is your company doing? The key position is vitally important. If it collapses we must do something about it early tomorrow."

The major ducked. A low flying plane roared overhead. Above the scream of its engine came a string of sharp reports—bullets spraying the street. The major did not drop the receiver. He replied as if he were sitting comfortably with crossed legs at his office desk. "I seem to remember already having told you twice that we have never had a direct communication line to the advanced position. There is only a cross line to the infantry's field radio on our right flank, and that does not answer. It takes a runner two hours to get here from the front line. Even if one arrived, which I don't consider likely under the circumstances, his information would already be out of date."

The speaker at Division Headquarters waited for a crackle on the line to subside. He cleared his throat. "Obviously you are in a difficult position but it's not up to the division to solve your problems. You must see that you get through all right. When you know anything for certain call me back." He sounded impatient and eager to finish the conversation.

The major bit his lip. "I shall get through all right," he said ambiguously, "but it's obviously the division's duty to give us artillery support. That's all I want from you." His voice had grown cutting. "My company must be aware by now that something is happening to them. Furthermore the other three companies of my battalion have been attached to other units and I have no reinforcements. It's high time to give us some artillery support. Since the division hasn't given the artillery permission to fire I'm telephoning, and I'll go on telephoning you as long as the line remains intact. You can be certain of that whether you like it or not."

"Don't be so childish, Schnitzer." Again that crackle on the line. "It's three o'clock in the morning. On your behalf I woke the general's orderly and he passed on your request. I've also given you his reply but that doesn't mean I'm going to wake the general up every time you call. You don't understand how things function at Division Headquarters. You only see things from your standpoint because you are in the middle of it all, but here . . ." The voice in the receiver swelled and screamed but that was due only to the transmission: "here everything takes its usual course and I can't step out of line on your behalf."

"Is that so?" said the major grimly. "Then I've only one more question to ask."

"Go ahead."

"Am I talking to the division or to a nuthouse?"

"I beg your pardon?" The voice in the receiver seemed to come through a wall.

"Nothing!" said the major hanging up. The room had grown bright from the glow of the fire outside. A figure stood outlined against the door.

"What do you want?"

A faint humming in the air grew louder until it became a roar. It whistled and hissed over the roof. The shell burst in the middle of the village street.

"What do you want?" repeated the major. Clods of earth rattled like hailstones on the roof.

The sergeant major reported as though he had been sent for. He stepped smartly forward from the door into the bright glare of the fire.

The major stared at the man as if he were an apparition. "Sergeant Major!"

"Yes, sir?"

"What is happening at the key position?"

The N.C.O. hesitated. The major saw his quivering face, took a bottle from the table and handed it to him.

"Have a drink first."

In the village street a voice came nearer, calling in a whining tone: "Stretcher bearer, stretcher bearer!"

The man ran past the house. The sergeant major took the bottle and drank greedily. The light of the flames flickered over his face and it was a long time before he put the bottle down. Then he looked at the major as if he had nothing to say.

"Well?" The major could not contain his impatience a moment longer.

"The Russians have attacked," said the sergeant major, as though this would account for his sudden appearance.

The major hesitated. He seemed to be waiting for the report and when the N.C.O. persisted in his silence he said helpfully: "What is your commanding officer's message?"

"Yes, sir. . . ." The sergeant major looked around the room and began to sweat.

"Are you sick?" asked the major.

"No . . . maybe . . . I guess so."

"You're overtired," said the major. "We all are." Like a doctor he took the man's wrist and felt the beating pulse. His hand brushed against the cold metal case of a wrist watch. "Well, now please give me the details. Pull yourself together. You're bringing the first report from the front line. Is the company holding out?"

"I don't know," whined the sergeant major.

There was a loud explosion just outside the hut. A blast swept through the room. The beams threatened to collapse. The smoke cleared. The window frames had been smashed and had fallen to the ground. The major wiped the dust out of his good eye. Maps, broken glass and papers lay scattered all over the room. The sergeant major was crouching on the floor.

"Are you hit?" asked the major.

The sergeant major stood up and said: "Report from the company. After strong artillery preparation the enemy launched an attack on the key position. The company is still holding out, but needs replacements urgently."

The major gave him a keen look. "Man, we're not on maneuvers now," he said, cutting the air with his hand as though he were cracking a riding whip. "For God's sake tell me how strong the Russians are. Are they attacking with tanks? Are we short of ammunition? Are our casualties heavy? Tell me everything you saw until the moment you left." The major broke off. "But tell me, when did you actually leave the company?"

The sergeant major gave an almost imperceptible start. "My watch has stopped," he said.

The major shook his head. Someone outside cried: "Where's the aid station?"

The major leaned out of the window: a man with a clumsily bandaged head. A little further off in the smoke another soldier hobbling on a stick with his arm in a sling.

"What unit?" asked the major.

The man with the head wound saw his shoulder straps and drew himself up a little. "Hartmann Infantry Regiment. Light machine gunner."

"When did you leave your unit?"

"Why did I leave my unit?"

"When?" shouted the major. "I said *when*."

"A good half an hour ago, sir."

"Your unit's on the right flank of the hill, isn't it?"

"Yes, Major."

"Then you couldn't have left it only half an hour ago."

"Yes, sir. A truck brought us back."

"When did the Russian attack start?"

"About eleven o'clock last night, sir."

"The attack. Not the artillery bombardment."

A fighter plane roared over the rooftops flying in the direction of the front line. The machine gun rattled wildly and the major could see the red stars on the wing. The man with the bandaged arm rolled himself into a ball on the ground. The major ducked beneath the window sill. The man with the head wound pressed against the wall of the hut. When it was over he bobbed up again.

"The pigs haven't attacked yet," he said bitterly.

"Do you mean to say that half an hour ago the Russians hadn't yet gone over to the attack?"

"Not on our front, sir, nor on the right and left, nor against the hill, or we should have seen them."

"Are you positive?" asked the major with great persistence.

"Yes, sir."

"Thank you. There's a first aid post at the end of the village."

The major turned back to the room and called: "Sergeant major!"

The room was empty.

"I can't understand it," he muttered pacing up and down. As if he were already out in the open. Around him the bare walls. The beamed ceiling. Only the roof kept him from seeing the sky. Alternate gusts of cold and warm air blew through the broken windows. And always the crackle and roar of flames.

There was a buzz in the brown telephone box which had fallen over on his desk.

"Schnitzer's Headquarters!"

The familiar voice from Division replied: "Merely wanted to tell you that the artillery has permission to fire."

"Thanks for the information." The major's voice was icy.

"That's all right. We're in it too now."

"What am I to understand by that?"

"Heavy enemy shelling at Emga. We've just been bombed."

"Things have gone pretty fast."

"Yes. It's a bit of a surprise. Things are getting lively up here too!"

"I'm delighted to hear it."

"Afraid I can't say the same," came the voice in the receiver. It had a strange ring. "We're moving out."

"What did you say?"

"Divisional Headquarters is moving back."

"I don't find your joke very funny," said the major with a frown.

"Unfortunately it's not a joke," replied the voice. "One of the facts that show how things are going here."

"But you can't withdraw the division in the middle of a battle."

"The division is not being withdrawn. It's remaining where it is. Your company has strict orders to hold the hill at all costs. Our headquarters, however, is being moved back a little. Those are the general's orders. Incidentally, he was in his pajamas when he got into the car. Perhaps you'll find that interesting."

"Unbelievable."

"Yes," said the bored voice after a pause. "Do you know why I'm telling you all this?"

"I don't quite understand, after our last conversation."

"You will shortly. I have a personal order for you."

"Yes?"

"You are to go up to the front line immediately to set an example for the fighting troops."

"Are these your own words?" Shells roared over the hut.

"No, the words of a general in his pajamas. Maybe he got them out of some story book." The shells burst in the village. "Those pigs!" said the voice at the other end of the line. "I just wanted you to know for whom you're sticking your neck out."

"Encouraging, isn't it?"

"Very." The officer at Division Headquarters lowered his voice. "I've only just understood why you kept pestering me for artillery. It isn't right that it's always only the decent ones who should die. A little hint at the right moment. . . ."

"Of course," said the major. "I won't go up to the front

line because the general wants it but rather because there may still be a few decent fellows left up there. Maybe I can be of some use to them. Whenever we do anything decent it's for the benefit of the decent ones. Maybe that consoles you a bit. You want a bit of consolation, don't you?"

A crackling came from the bakelite receiver, but no reply.

"Hello, hello!" called the major banging twice on the cradle, but the line was dead. Thoughtfully he replaced the receiver. He went out into the smoke-filled corridor where he found the adjutant crouching exhausted in a corner.

"What's happened?"

The adjutant shook his head and pointed to his sleeve. There was a huge tear in his uniform running from the shoulder to the cuff. "I was in the street when the fighters came over," he explained distractedly.

"You're lucky," said the major absentmindedly. "I have to go up to the line. You take charge of the battalion."

"What do you mean, sir?" The adjutant stared uncomprehendingly. But the door had already slammed and the major had disappeared into a cloud of smoke. The heat struck him in the face. Somewhere in the village, small arms ammunition was exploding. He ran behind the hut to his car.

"The front line!" he ordered the driver. The engine started at once. The smoke lay against the windshield like a grey cloth. Things were better as soon as they had left the burning village. They drove eastward towards the blazing horizon. The sand hissed beneath the tires and they put on speed. When they came to the cemetery a huge shell hole suddenly yawned in their path.

The driver gripped the steering wheel, the brakes screamed, the major was flung against the windshield. He closed his eyes. The car nearly turned over and for a moment he was terrified. They came to a standstill between the rows of crosses. The vehicle quivered like a beast at bay.

"What do we do now?" asked the driver dully.

"Drive through the cemetery!"

The crosses banged against the bumpers and the wheels sank into the graves. The major felt uncomfortable. Just before they reached the road again two planes shot silently from behind the treetops. The engines began to drone. The planes zoomed steeply, banked and returned to the attack. They had spotted the grey car among the white crosses. Small red flames spurted through the propellers. Earth sprayed up. The driver already was flat on the ground in front of the radiator. The major as though frozen to stone stared up into the sky at the two diving cockpits. Bullets ate a patch towards the car. The beechwood crosses splintered. The air became unbearably hot—then a sharp whirl of drumbeats, and the metal of the car was shot full of holes. The noise of the engines died away and the graveyard was peaceful once more as though nothing had happened. A leaden morning sky lay over the swaying grass. Peace and solitude. Even the burning village fitted into the picture. In the distance a charred scaffolding collapsed but no sound came from it. In front of the car the driver lay motionless in the grass. A white liquid trickled from the back of his head. The major laid the dead man on his back. He found it difficult to close the staring eyes. The memory of his child came back again. Something painful, mingled with rage and helplessness. He bent down trying to say some kind of prayer but he could not think of any words. One memory dogged his mind. What had happened twenty five years ago seemed like yesterday. . . .

The bell rang and the landlady came in. "There's a lady to see you." The lady came in. "I've been told that you were my son's last company commander. Private Lotz— he's missing." "Missing? There must be a mistake." The woman smiled through her tears. "I knew it. He's alive. He must be somewhere in a hospital. The letters must have gone astray. The revolution . . . it's terrible. Do you know anything about him?" Striped wallpaper. A green lampshade. Paint peeling from the double windows. Shall I tell her that he's dead? Her face is wrinkled. Someone has taken a nail and ruined a work of art—drawn countless furrows in that face. He was her only child. "I'm afraid I can't tell you very much. He was wounded." "Yes, and then?" "We brought him back. The revolution. . . . In the fighting. . . . You understand. You'll be sure to get news soon." A wounded man hung in the barbed wire. The stretcher bearer was shot through the head as he tried to fetch him. The company commander forbade all attempts at rescue before nightfall. By evening the wounded man was dead. "You were his company commander, weren't you?" "Yes." The mother wept. "When your son writes to you please let me know." The woman left with tears in her eyes.

The major stood up and looked around him. Over the farthest front line, black and menacing, lay the storm of battle. The remains of the company were fighting in the key position. Somewhere wives were waiting for their husbands and children for their fathers. He remembered his useless order to attack the railway embankment. With sullen determination he left the cemetery choosing the shortest way to the front line—the road through the marsh.

Chapter Six

THE sergeant major stood behind a tree and watched the figures swarming in front of the artillery colonel's house. The roof was blazing fiercely and in a few moments it would obviously collapse. Soldiers were carrying cases, crates and furniture into the open air. A basket of crockery swayed perilously. Articles of uniform were passed from hand to hand. A few men, trying to put out the fire, lugged buckets of water from the well and emptied them over the smoldering beams.

The sergeant major recognized the sooty faces. He noticed, too, that the Russian artillery fire had shifted further west. The shells now howled over the ruins of the village. They were bursting near the saw mill in the forest, in the dense growth of trees.

He came out of his hiding place and looked carefully around. No one had noticed him. He made his way hesitatingly along the street, made a detour around some low bushes and approached the burning house. Crates and baggage lay scattered about the weed-filled garden. The exhausted men stood in clusters and looked at the collapsing frame. There was no officer in sight so the sergeant major approached with a firm tread. An energetic movement of the hand and he barked: "You can't leave that stuff lying about there."

The men stared at him in amazement, noticed his rank and began to put some order into the muddle.

"Bring it over here," ordered the sergeant major taking a small table with a chessboard inlay and carrying it to the place he had indicated. Men from the artillery, he realized, and felt somewhat out of place. When a car turned in from the road he immediately recognized the colonel. "Carry on!" he cried. He went over, raised his hand smartly to his steel helmet and tried to report.

"Good, good," said the colonel absent-mindedly, looking with disgust at the remains of his house. "Can you get a truck for my things?" He stuck his monocle in his eye and scrutinized the sergeant major. "Oh, an engineer! Nice of you," he growled, as he saw the black collar tabs. "Thanks all the same but we can manage on our own."

The sergeant major wanted to say something but the colonel turned his back on him and gave the necessary orders. The sergeant major walked away. What should he do now? The village street was empty. He sidled across it and inspected it again from the other side. An officer appeared from among the ruins. The N.C.O. drew himself to attention, gave the impression that he had something important to do, saluted and went by. He felt the officer's gaze in his back and quickened his pace until he reached the highway. A *panje* cart came towards him at full speed.

The driver was standing up in his seat with the reins slack. He did not even look at the sergeant major but disappeared into the village raising a cloud of dust.

There was some undergrowth nearby. The sergeant major thought for a moment and decided to remain in the road. A car shot out from behind a bend making towards him. He leapt out of the way. The vehicle stopped and an officer leaned out.

"Have you come from the front? I've got to close a gap with my battalion and I can't find my bearings." He gave the sergeant major no time to speak. "Podrowa. Am I on the right road?"

"Yes, sir." He pointed to the direction from which he had just come. The smoking village already lay out of sight behind the edge of the wood. "Only half a mile."

"Thank you. Where are you off to?"

"To division," he said looking the officer straight in the face. The car drove off. The sergeant major went on his way but now paid close attention to the road. As soon as he spotted a new cloud of dust in the distance he jumped quickly into the wood and took cover behind a bush. Men on the march, clanking tools, muffled voices. Through the foliage he could see only their feet. Infantry, obviously. Then the wheels of armored cars. Probably heavy machine guns. A pause and then more pairs of boots. A whole company. More wheels, probably light machine guns this time. At last, silence.

The sergeant major waited and then returned to the road. He kept close to the side of the wood. From the direction of Podrowa, explosions of heavy artillery. The shells whirred over him. Behind him was the faint drumming of the front line. A figure appeared. The sergeant major hesitated and then went on. It was a straggler, sweating profusely and carrying a wireless apparatus on his back. His steel helmet was wobbling on his head and wisps of hair had fallen down on his face. He tried to pass but the sergeant major stopped him.

"Hello! Where you going?"

The man put down his transmitter wearily and wiped the sweat from his forehead on his sleeve. "Radio reserve," he said sulkily. "I've got to get to the artillery at Podrowa. One of the sets there is out of action."

"Where have you come from?"

"Somewhere over there in the woods," he said pointing vaguely behind him. "They called us up. I've got to get going."

"Tough luck," said the sergeant major offering the man a cigarette. "Any news of the fighting troops?"

"Plenty."

"How do things look?"

The man did not seem very communicative. He made a vague gesture and said: "Pretty messed up."

"Any details?"

"The Russians have broken through. Anyone that can still run is running."

The sergeant major gave him the opened cigarette packet. "Here take these."

"Thanks." The man became more communicative.

"There's a rumor they're going to draw the front line back to the five-point crossroads, but I've no idea where that is."

"To the left of the high ground."

"Never heard of it."

"The highway leads to Podrowa. It swings around down below here."

"Highway," said the soldier picking up his apparatus. "For me it's only a damned path in the woods."

"Good luck!" said the sergeant major and went on his way. Things don't look too bad, he thought. He would have to be careful. He could safely remain on the road. In this muddle who could tell whether he had orders or not? In Emga he would go to Supply Headquarters. That was his duty. There would be plenty to do there. Collect stragglers. Double rations for the company. Perhaps even chocolate. They would certainly be able to use him. He walked on, deep in thought.

He did not notice the soldier lolling against a tree. A shadow suddenly entered his consciousness.

"Sergeant major!"

He turned around with a start.

"Just a moment!"

The sergeant major noticed the corporal's stripes. "What's the matter? Have you gone crazy?"

The corporal came calmly up to him and said: "Where you going?"

The sergeant was puzzled. Such a thing had never happened to him before. "I don't like your tone, man," he said.

He wanted to say more but something warned him and he started to walk on. The corporal caught his arm. His grip was surprisingly tight.

"Damn it!" He freed himself from the grip, more perplexed than angry. Then he noticed a metal disc on the corporal's chest. He fell silent. "Well, at last," said the corporal sourly. "Military Police. Your pass, please!"

The sergeant major grew unsure of himself. He had a sinking feeling in his stomach. His hand trembled as he unbuttoned his breast pocket. I hope he doesn't notice it, he thought. "I suppose you think I'm a spy?" he said, trying to joke. The corporal looked him up and down as he rather guiltily handed him his pay book.

"Marching orders?"

"Haven't got any." He was surprised how easily that had come out.

"Where are you from and where are you going?" asked the corporal looking him straight in the eyes.

"My company's on the hill in the key position. I've been sent to Supply Headquarters at Emga." He was too excited to weigh his words. What he said was in line with the plan he had settled on just a few minutes before. He could not think of anything better. He tried to calm himself but he felt as though he were being strangled.

"What do you want at Supply Headquarters?" A strange note had crept into the corporal's voice.

"As a sergeant major I belong to supply." What rubbish, he thought in surprise.

"Not necessarily."

The sergeant major began to cough and the corporal waited politely until he had finished.

"When did you leave your company and the hill position?"

Now if I can only find the right answer, he thought. His reply could prove decisive but his head was in a whirl. Shall I say before or after? Before seemed the better of the two but what about the time in between? Suddenly an idea crossed his mind. He would run away, but the corporal had a revolver. The holster was unfastened and the butt was sticking out. He abandoned the idea.

"Midnight," he replied firmly.

"I suppose you think we don't know when the Russian bombardment started?"

What does that mean, the sergeant major wondered. He thought things over for a moment.

"Naturally, some time before," he said trying to make things look better.

"Right," said the corporal sarcastically. "Come with me." He pushed the sergeant major around unceremoniously and made him walk ahead toward a clearing in the wood. The sergeant major could not help thinking of the Russian prisoner. He remembered the words: "A bullseye." The night had started with the prod he had given the Russian and with this prod in his own back it had come to an end.

In the clearing stood a car. Now for the first time he saw the trace of tires on the ground. I should have been more careful, he thought. Three military police were leaning by the car smoking. Their steel helmets lay on the ground. He saw that they were a lieutenant, a sergeant major and a sergeant.

"Well, Mayer, you old snooper. What have you brought us?" said the lieutenant with a laugh.

"Something a little suspicious. We ought to look into it." The corporal spoke as if there were no such thing as difference in ranks. I shall be able to talk to the lieutenant, thought the sergeant major. He made an effort to make a good impression, stood to attention and saluted.

"Herr Leutnant, I have. . . ."

"Psht! With me you don't speak unless you are asked," said the lieutenant calmly.

The corporal reached into the sergeant major's breast pocket, removed the pay book and handed it to the lieutenant, who began to turn the pages slowly. "He maintains that he left the position at midnight. It's been confirmed that the Russian bombardment had already started at that time. Wants to go to Supply Headquarters at Emga," said the corporal. He stressed the word midnight.

"Come on, admit you took a powder," said the lieutenant casually.

"Herr Leutnant. . . ."

"Yes or no? No fairy tales." His manner was very disturbing.

"No, sir."

"What was your job with the company?" asked the lieutenant and smoothed a dogear on a page of the pay book. "Company troop leader." The sergeant major thought: I always made my own duty entries and let the captain confirm the dates.

"And then your C.O., in the middle of a bombardment, just before an attack, sends you down to Supply Headquarters?"

The sergeant major bit his lip.

"I think we've got one of them," said the lieutenant turning to the sergeant.

The corporal nodded. "It doesn't always have to be a private, you see."

"Crazy business," added the sergeant ambiguously.

The sergeant major felt sick.

"Well, we'd better get going," said the lieutenant, standing up. "Take him to Emga."

"Yes, sir." A hand took the sergeant major's arm and led him gently to the car. The corporal took his place at the wheel.

"You're to return immediately."

"Yes, sir."

They drove out of the clearing in the direction of Emga.

"Things won't be so bad," said the sergeant offering him a cigarette. The corporal slowed down so the match would not blow out. The sergeant major puffed deeply on the cigarette. "Perhaps you've been lucky," said the sergeant. The corporal put his foot down on the accelerator again. The sergeant major thought they were behaving as though he could be locked up for this business. He cast a glance at the speedometer. The needle hovered at about forty miles an hour. They stopped twice to let other vehicles pass. The drivers glanced at the sergeant major with curiosity.

Emga. A broad main street and log huts. A church without a roof on a small hill. Away to the right a house on fire. The car bumped over railway lines. Behind a smoking engine a railway car with whitewashed windows and a big red cross in the center. Standards and flags with various regimental emblems had been stuck into the ground. A fountain of earth was thrown up in the middle of the street. The sergeant major had not heard the whine of the shell above the noise of the locomotive. He ducked. To their left lay a long rambling building with a lopsided divisional emblem above the entrance. Soldiers were bringing out documents and loading them onto armored trucks. Behind the low wooden fence figures wrapped in blankets lay on stretchers. The car pulled up before a barn that looked like an ancient watch tower. The plaster was crumbling from the outer walls. At the door stood a military policeman.

"Get going," said the sergeant jumping out of the car, "before the Russian gunners get us." He waited impatiently for the sergeant major. The entrance was so low they both had to duck. It was rather dark inside and a cold draft swept through the building. There was no window to be seen in the barn but a little light trickled in through the cracks in the wall. With an experienced hand a sergeant with a face like a prize fighter relieved him of his revolver and belt. He had no time to protest. Moreover he realized it would have been pointless. He must wait. Later he would have a reckoning with them. He was given a cardboard disc with a number, and his name was entered in a rather dilapidated book. The sergeant pushed him up some stairs. Above them was an iron grating with a large meshed door in it. The sergeant unlocked it, made way for the sergeant major to enter and then tramped down the stairs again. Empty paper bags caught his eye. DEUTSCHER PORTLAND ZEMENT. Around him damp brick walls. Three soldiers sat on the wooden floor playing cards. They had made up a pack from scraps of paper ripped off the bags. Their uniforms were covered with cement dust. Overhead, beams and slats and the underside of the red roof tiles. A pale light trickled through the chinks.

"The last trump!" The men had not taken notice of him. One of them spat on the floor. On his arm the sergeant major could see the marks of torn off corporal's stripes. "Perhaps he can tell us something. When are the Russians coming?"

The sergeant major made no reply.

"He's shy." They shuffled the cards.

Their laughter was oppressive. "And which commandment have you broken? The eighth?"

"You can cut that out," said the sergeant major. Now he caught sight of still another figure crouching against the wall.

"Would the sergeant major be so kind as to inform us when the Russians will finally get to Emga?" mocked the demoted corporal. "It's damned important for us."

"Perhaps for him too," said one of the others.

102

A shell exploded in the village. They listened attentively and the sergeant major tried to discover in what direction the front lay. He was unsuccessful. The soldier went on taunting him.

"We're not respectable enough company for him. A sergeant major can't possibly get off his high horse."

The sergeant major ignored the remark. He made an effort to control himself and began to look at the man huddled up against the wall. He was seething was rage. It was all a big mistake. After all he had his captain's permission to go back to the rear; he had reported to the major and had wanted to go to Emga. Obviously. Where else should he have gone? It was all a mistake. Loud explosions outside once more. Mud and splinters rattled on the roof and the chalk trickled down the walls. Hell, he thought, at any moment we can get a direct hit. I'm locked in and all on account of a mistake. He must speak to an officer at once but he must think out in advance what he should say. With all this din going on he could not collect his thoughts.

"Well, Mr. Innocent. You must have come from the rear or else you'd open your mouth."

"Shut your trap!" shouted the sergeant major abruptly. They fell silent but it was only a few seconds before their laughter rang out again. The corporal was bent double as though he had the cramps. But there was something disturbing in his laughter. Fear and hatred. Suddenly he stopped. A face strained bright red glared at the sergeant major.

"You bastards have run roughshod over us all so far but

this is the end of it, do you understand?" The veins on his forehead stood out and he approached the sergeant major like a beast of prey. "I'll never get out of this lousy hole and I don't want to. The whole damned swindle's over for me. I'm not going to let myself be treated like a dog any more." His voice grew hoarser and the sergeant major recoiled. Step by step the corporal drove him into the corner. He could see an angry red scar on the man's forehead. He felt with his hands along the wall. The scar drew closer. "Help, sergeant!" he cried.

The corporal's fist struck him in the face and made him reel. A gurgle came from his throat. A second blow. He did not even dare to raise his arms. He slumped against the wall and closed his eyes. Suddenly as though through a veil he heard a voice say: "I guess you haven't had enough!" A swishing sound. The sergeant major tried to open his eyes. The M.P. was in the room and was hitting the demoted corporal with a riding crop. Blow after blow rained down at random on his head and shoulders. "You bastard!" The corporal collapsed and the other prisoners huddled against the wall. The sergeant major felt satisfaction. He put out his foot and kicked the corporal in the belly.

The M.P. whirled around. "Hey, you!" he said and raised his whip.

The sergeant major shrunk back. "He hit me." He felt relief when he noticed that the sergeant was not going to strike.

"Keep your trap shut!" he said. "You're all alike here."

"I'll make you pay for that," hissed the sergeant major.

He could have bitten off his tongue but the other looked at him in sheer amazement. That's the way I must talk to him, thought the sergeant major. "Open the door at once," he ordered.

"What?" exclaimed the sergeant.

"Open the door, I said."

There was a loud explosion just outside the barn. Plaster fell off the walls. It seemed as though the roof would be blown off. For a moment the room was as bright as day and pieces of tile rained down on them.

By the time it was quiet again the M.P. had already clumped down the steps, leaving behind him an atmosphere of uncomfortable letdown. Patches of sunlight lit up the floor which was strewn with cement and bits of tile. The two prisoners stood up and dragged the corporal into the shade. They looked like rumpled vultures squatting in a ruin after their prey had been taken away from them. They looked with hatred at the sergeant major whose glance shifted nervously until it fell on the man who had not moved during the altercation. He was a very young boy and he was still leaning against the wall. His uniform sagged over his narrow shoulders. A pair of skinny hands, a head that seemed too heavy for his body. Deep set eyes under the unruly hair. The sergeant major sat down circumspectly next to him in the shadow of the wall. The coolness and the dim light made him feel calmer.

"Are you sick?" he asked in such a quiet voice that the soldier could hardly understand him.

The youngster nodded almost imperceptibly. He kept his

eyes fixed on a certain spot—a white patch of damp on the opposite wall.

"How long have you been here?" asked the sergeant major gently.

"I don't know."

"You must know."

Another silence. Then the boy went on: "They always take me along with them. It's been a long time now."

The sergeant major started. He had never seen such eyes. The pupils looked dead as though the man were blind. However they moved and took in his shoulder tabs.

"You're a sergeant major. . . ."

"Yes. Have you been sentenced?" Perhaps he could hear something that would prove useful to him.

"Not yet," said the boy.

"You're waiting for it, eh?"

"Yes." He continued to stare straight ahead of him. The three other men in the cell watched them.

"What did you do?"

"I hid."

"Hid?" whispered the sergeant major.

"We were supposed to attack the Russian trenches and I hid because of my mother."

The sergeant major was disappointed. He would have been satisfied had it been from fear.

"She's alone and she only has me. Do you understand that?"

The sergeant major looked at the skinny body, the bony fingers and the yellow skin of the cheek bones. Suddenly he said: "You'll certainly never see your mother again."

"That all depends on the God," replied the youth clearly.

"What God?"

"That one there." He pointed down below. He meant the M.P.

"He's no God," replied the sergeant major with a wry smile.

"We're all in his hands." His eyes began to blink. The sergeant major felt uncomfortable and turned aside.

"Idiot," came a voice from the other side of the cell.

"You'll soon see!" The shrill boyish voice rang excitedly through the barn. It made the sergeant major shudder.

"Have you a watch?" asked one of the three men on the other side.

"It's eight o'clock," he replied almost gratefully.

"So the day's only just beginning."

Chapter Seven

"ATTENTION, attention, all stations. From 0801 hours to 0810 hours we are transmitting the time in clear," came a voice from somewhere in a forest far behind the front—a voice speaking into the microphone of a short wave transmitter. The transmitting impulses ran through wires, tubes and coils, clambered up a thin copper wire to a tall pole and then through an aerial into the ether. "Attention, attention, all stations. . . ."

"Corps is sending out the time," said an officer in a radio car at Division Headquarters. "Make all apparatus ready to receive. Interrupt transmissions." The operators switched over and tuned in with their knobs. Synchronization of watches. They received the incoming voice on their wave lengths.

". . . the time in clear," heard the operator at Podrowa. He cast a glance at his watch. They'll transmit that now for nine minutes he thought. They would do better to listen to me, to what I have to transmit:

Position highway eastern exit Podrowa—contact with

unit broken—enemy mortar fire on Podrowa—retreat along highway—no longer according to plan—can recognize infantry, artillery, antiaircraft—no weapons, no trucks, no officers—no complete units—leaderless troops—wounded officer informed me Russian pincer movement around Hill 308—hill presumably still in our hands—end of message.

"One minute past eight," announced the voice in his receiving set and blocked the wavelengths.

"Two minutes past eight," heard the wireless operator at the five-point crossroads. He had no time to look at his watch and did not interrupt his transmission. Within a radius of two miles every operator heard his report together with the official Corps time:

"Here Saturn—waiting in vain for promised reserve battalion—Russian tanks ahead in unascertainable strength—defense collapsed—enemy break-through on a wide front north of our own position—resistance our troops flagging—on Hill 308 two enemy tanks without infantry—further resistance impossible here for lack of ammunition—blowing up my apparatus—end of message! end! end!"

"Three minutes past eight," he still heard. Then the apparatus flew up in the air like the cork from a bottle of champagne.

The major wiped the mud from his wrist watch. Four minutes past eight. So he had already been in the marsh over an hour. The whole time up to his knees in water and twice in it up to his chest. He had lost one boot and his revolver was full of mud. Compass broken. Both shoulder straps torn off by branches. He looked like a wild beast. I must go on, on, he thought. His hands were bleeding. He could already hear their machine guns. Perhaps another three hundred yards to go and then he would be with his men. . . .

The lieutenant in one of the Russian tanks on the hill turned the knob of his radio set. "Five minutes past eight," said a German voice in his headphones. He understood no German. Through the observation slit he watched the Siberians. They had cleared a length of the German trench and had now been caught in a trap. Thirty Germans sat in a hedgehog position at the foot of the hill and controlled the whole sector. The Russian tanks were wheeling beyond the marsh. Each time the infantry behind them forged ahead they came under fire from the German machine guns and were mowed down. He looked at his watch. The position was becoming untenable. He had already been three hours on the hill. His ammunition bins were empty. Why didn't the engineers lay a new carpet? His own artillery was firing on the hill. The shrapnel rattled against the steel walls and he could not even get out of the tank. For an hour he had been here with his engine cut off next to the skeleton of the high tension pylon. He could not wait up here for ever. The hole under the concrete support of the high tension pylon looked like a dugout entrance. An empty tin lay on the parapet. Only his own artillery fire prevented him from getting out and looking.

"Six minutes past eight," rang in his ears; it was the German voice which he did not understand.

"Six minutes past eight," said the sergeant, sticking his head cautiously over the parapet. The sun glistened in the puddles in front of the trenches. Behind the torn barbed wire he could see the outlines of the Russian tanks. Brown heaps everywhere; broken limbs pointing to the sky. A shot rang out from his own trench and hit the tank turret, grazing the steel. Madman, he thought. He is trying to shoot through the observation slit.

"Stop that nonsense!" he shouted down the trench. "Otherwise they'll retaliate."

The runner came out of his hole and leaned against the opposite wall of the trench. He raised his clenched fists in the air and said: "What are they waiting for?" To the right and left of the high tension pylon the two tanks stood motionless.

"That antitank squad isn't worth a crap!"

"They've run out!" The runner spat into the trench. "Those bastards have taken a powder!"

In the marsh behind the tanks there was a sudden movement. The sergeant looked more closely.

"We ought to lengthen the sap to the C.O.'s dugout— then we'll have room to move."

The sergeant did not reply. A Red soldier sprang from behind one tank and ran across to the next one.

"We've been written off," said the runner staring up into the sky. "They haven't sent us even one goddamned plane."

The Russian ran along the damaged barbed wire between the tanks. An enamel mess kit glittered on his hip. He was waving his arms.

"I have to get out of this hole," declared the runner. "These wounded men are driving me crazy."

On the enemy side, by the barbed wire in front of the second tank, the Russian suddenly turned around and jumped back.

"Maybe the best thing for us to do. . . ." The runner's voice paused for a moment, "would be to surrender."

"Do you think so?" The sergeant looked at him out of the corner of his eye.

"If we only knew what would happen then. . . ." There was a sudden activity behind the tanks. "They're coming," he shouted. The runner leapt back into his foxhole. The two machine guns to right and left began to rattle.

The sergeant thought: they attack right on the half hour. Unwittingly he looked at his watch. Seven minutes past eight.

Eight minutes past eight. The Russian colonel ran his ruler nervously over the map spread out on the table.

"Pity." His adjutant shrugged his shoulders and said: "The carpet broke under the third tank and the infantry got stuck. That was the end." He pointed to the map, to a number in the black circle. "The position of Sostschenko's battalion is very serious."

A draft of air turned up the edge of the map. The door had sprung open.

"How heavy are our casualties?" The colonel turned round and looked out of the window. A girl stood there in the road. Her hair fluttered in the wind.

"We don't know anything so far," said the adjutant. He listened. From the neighboring room they could hear the general's voice.

"Do we know that girl?" asked the colonel pointing at the figure outside.

"What girl?" The adjutant purposely looked over her head.

"Whom she belongs to, I mean," said the colonel reproachfully.

"Captain Sostschenko."

The colonel nodded. "As far as I know one of the first aid stations has asked for help."

"Yes, Comrade Colonel."

The corporal pushed the detonator into the mine. It was quiet in the hole. He could hear the metal detonator rubbing against the mine. He could see neither the face nor the hands on his watch dial; the phosphorous had worn off.

"What are you doing there?" came a voice out of the darkness. "We don't want to pay for your irresponsibility with our lives."

"Everyone can do what he likes," replied the corporal. "I, for example, am about to blow up a Russian tank."

"There are two of them," said the voice, "and the second one will. . . ."

"Don't talk such rubbish." Once more the detonator scraped against the metal.

"You're not really going to do it, are you?" asked the voice. Now it was trembling.

"I've thought it over for half an hour," replied the corporal casually. Without making any noise he drew up his legs and pulled his back up slowly against the wall. The mine was heavy.

Across from him there was a movement. A hand tried to grasp his arm. He gave it a heavy blow. Two hands tried to grab his shoulders. He raised a knee and repelled them with all his strength. There was a cry of pain. He caught a whiff of bad breath as he sprang to the exit. Holding the mine in his right hand he tried to hoist himself out of the hole with his left. For the first time he noticed that his limbs were stiff and that he had no strength in them. In addition to this the daylight blinded him.

"You're crazy! Stay here!" screamed a desperate voice behind him.

His head was now out of the hole. Then someone caught his feet and held them in an iron grip. He must free himself. Five steps away from him towered the clay-stained wall of the tank. A shapeless caterpillar belt, screw heads and rivets. He struggled with all his might. Trying to lift the mine over the hole. Trying to roll it toward the tank. The hands still held him fast as in a vise and his strength slowly ebbed. "Let me go," he moaned, clutching the mine to his chest. He could no longer breathe. A little hatch opened in the wall of the tank. A barrel like the spout of a watering can was aimed at his head. With his last strength he tore the safety cord from the mine.

At that moment an oily liquid began to trickle from the barrel of the flame thrower. A harmless spark flickered. Suddenly red hot flames licked his face. His head burnt like a match. The mine began to glow. There was a powerful explosion: the corporal did not exist any more. The blast swept through the hole. It beat against the earthen walls and against the concrete. Flames ran to the other mines. Papers, uniforms and flesh became charred instantaneously. The explosives which had caught fire lifted the lump of concrete into the air and blew the skeleton of the pylon sky high.

The lieutenant in his tank heard the foreign voice once more in his earphones; then the turret began to turn with him inside it. The steel casing burst. The voice said for the last time: "Ten minutes past eight," but he did not hear it any more.

Somewhere far behind the front line a hand threw a switch. Little lamps went out and the tubes cooled down. From the east new transmissions went their complicated way.

Chapter Eight

THREE MOVEMENTS had saved the lives of the captain and the wounded man in the dugout—not for ever, but at least for a time. The captain could no longer decide whether he had done the right thing or not. It had been instinctive. He had picked up a stone, wrapped his somewhat soiled white handkerchief around it and thrown it at the feet of the Red Army soldier who had suddenly appeared in the dugout entrance.

The lives of both of them at that moment hung by a thread. A man who has advanced across open country for three hundred yards under machine-gun fire and exploding hand grenades, then run for his life through a maze of enemy trenches, and at last stands in front of an enemy dugout with a live hand grenade that will explode in three seconds—such a man is only a machine. He might not see a white handkerchief wrapped around a stone. He might see it but think nothing of it. He might be intoxicated by a lust for blood. Or he might immediately realize what it means and throw his grenade in the dugout just the same because he does not know what to do with it. That the Russian threw his over the wall of the trench was pure chance and everything that followed was the result of this chance—above all the fact that the captain now sat as a prisoner in his own dugout.

The captain did not know how long it had been. His watch had disappeared together with several other things. In any case, it must have been hours. His nervousness had abated. He even felt a sort of peace. The critical moment seemed to be over. He knew from experience that as a general rule prisoners were shot only in the first excitement—at least here in his company. Furthermore, the Russians were not very different from his own men, merely other uniforms and other features. Otherwise they were just as filthy, just as weary and just as obedient. He could not be certain who commanded them but there was certainly some sense in what they did. They searched his dugout, distributed the bread, checked their weapons, made room for the wounded which other men brought in and also attended to his wounded comrade as though he were one of their own men. He rather admired their discipline. They were in the midst of a battle and they made every effort not to let this be seen. He almost envied the wounded man to whom they paid more attention than to him. The German lay between two wounded Russians on a wire bed, an overcoat rolled up under his head and covered with a canvas sheet. His arm had been bandaged quite professionally. They had found some chocolate; they brought it to their comrades and also stuck a piece in the German's mouth. There were plenty of candles burning now, which they had brought with them. The candles smelled a bit but there was light even in the remotest corners of the dugout.

Still—something seemed to have gone wrong. There was still shooting in the trench although the artillery fire had ceased. A machine gun kept hammering and in the distance he could hear the explosion of hand grenades. Nor was there any attempt to take him and the wounded man away. This disturbed him. He had already come to terms with his destiny. In his mind's eye he saw a prisoner-of-war camp, barbed wire and peace for the first time in months. No explosions, no shell holes, no orders and no responsibility. He found it a consoling thought. He would probably have to wait a long time for his release but he made up his mind that he would not be impatient. After all, he could learn their language and undertake some interesting studies. He remembered the lectures he had given his students on Russian ethnology. He was already beginning to think of peace-time activities. He had already started to feel remote from his present predicament.

"How do you do?" said a throaty voice near him. He looked up with surprise at a strange face and suddenly realized that the voice had spoken German. So it's the same with them as it is with us, he thought. All of us know a few words of the other language.

"Lieutenant Trupikow," said the Russian bowing correctly.

The captain was so surprised that he automatically stood up.

"Please remain seated," said the other most politely, with

an inviting motion toward a bench behind a wobbly table made of ammunition boxes. The captain sat down, somewhat bewildered.

"Our battalion has had the honor of attacking your position. Unfortunately not with complete success, as you are bound to have noticed."

The Russian took a tallow candle which had been stuck on a bayonet on the wall and placed it on the table. He had remarkably slender, well-groomed hands. "Will you have a cigarette?" he said taking out his case, opening it and handing it across the table.

"Thank you." With two fingers the captain took a cigarette. In the case was a German identification tag. He jerked back.

"From one of your men," said the Russian and went on quite unperturbed: "I should like a little information from you." He paused. "Naturally you are not compelled to answer if you consider it impracticable." He smiled and looked the captain straight in the eyes.

The German hesitated. A minute ago he would have been ready to admit anything. He was a prisoner and first of all he thought of himself. He would have surrendered to a sergeant. But now? The lieutenant's manner was disturbing. Now he must go on fighting, with other weapons. It was a matter of personal dignity.

"I'm in your hands," he said with as much self control as he could muster.

"Oh, this is no interrogation. Merely a personal question." The Russian glanced at the decorations on the captain's tunic. "Why do your men defend themselves so desperately?"

"But they're not defending themselves any more," replied the captain. The Russian's expression irritated him.

"You're wrong," smiled the lieutenant. "They're fighting like the devil. Up ahead in this same trench a squad has dug itself in and will not surrender. I should very much like to know why."

So that is the reason for the continued shooting, thought the captain.

"What section is it?" he asked. It interested him to know who it could be.

"It's difficult to say," replied the Russian. He reached for a canvas case which lay next to him on the bench and took out paper and pencil. The smile disappeared from his lips. "If this is the position"—he drew a vague line across the paper—"and here is the sap leading to your dugout, then it must be here. . . ." He pointed to a certain spot on the line.

"Between the saps, then?" said the captain.

"Oh, there's another trench!" said the Russian drawing a third line.

"And here is the communication trench," put in the captain, "and at this spot there's another dugout."

"Hmm," said the Russian glancing up quickly. "So they must be men of your unit, and they won't surrender."

"Is their position hopeless?" The captain looked at the sketch absentmindedly.

"Yes. We're already west of the hill and I'm certain that

your people know it. But they go on fighting and I can't understand why." Trupikow thought of the two tanks which a quarter of an hour ago had been blown into the air together with the concrete foundation and the skeleton of the high tension pylon. He knew that the hill was once more no-man's land. Presumably a German machine gun would soon begin to fire from up there.

"My company is composed of very simple people. Every High Command uses propaganda methods. Do you understand me? It's not easy for the men." The captain kept his eyes averted from the other man's face and stared fixedly into the flame of the candle.

"You mean they're afraid of being taken prisoner?"

"Yes. Perhaps people have the wrong idea."

"Oh, I understand," said the lieutenant with a smile. "At home people say that the Germans eat a lot of sauerkraut. I was very curious when I came to Germany but I can reassure you. They do not eat any more sauerkraut than we do."

"So you know Germany?" asked the captain with surprise.

"I'm a violinist and I studied there."

"Ah, I see." The captain looked at the Russian's well-groomed hands.

"You must excuse me for a moment," said Trupikow standing up. "Do you understand any Russian?"

"No."

The lieutenant went outside and gave a few words of command in his own language. Uneasily the captain realized that he had taken the sketch of the position with him.

He felt abandoned and betrayed. More disturbing than his failure to come to terms with God was the sudden collapse of his authority.

"I enjoyed myself in Germany," said the lieutenant on his return to the dugout as though he wanted to re-create the friendly atmosphere. But his face was strangely tense. "This will interest you. A single man has just come out of the marsh. He ran right through my troops and climbed into the trench with the surrounded men."

"Must be a deserter," said the captain shaking his head.

"He came from the rear or from the front," went on the Russian, "whichever you like. He disappeared before he could be . . ." He changed his mind and said: "before my men could do anything."

"Troops sometimes lose their heads," said the captain. He was thinking: we are colleagues for we are both interested in the arts.

"I agree," said the lieutenant, "but what am I to do if your people won't surrender? I have qualms. That's what you say isn't it?"

"Why?" The captain thought of the War Academy: sober exchange of ideas in front of the sand bags.

"We can't go on putting up with them for ever," said the lieutenant. "If they don't come to their senses. . . ."

"What would you do then?" A captain standing by the sandbags, checking the capacity of his lieutenant to make a decision.

Trupikow looked up quickly and said: "I hoped you would make some suggestion."

"Me?" The captain again felt like a prisoner.

"You could explain to your men the hopelessness of their position. It's really a question of saving human lives," said Trupikow staring seriously into the captain's face.

The captain lowered his eyes and stared once more into the small flame of the candle. "How would you interpret such action?"

"I give you my word as an officer that I would behave no differently if I were in your position."

"And your plan?"

"Very simple. We'll take you within calling distance of your troops. You will order them to surrender and tell them that I will ensure them honorable treatment."

"I'm an officer," replied the captain, "but I'll do it." He stood up.

"Don't misunderstand me," said the lieutenant politely, taking up his revolver. They went out together.

The captain's eyes were blinded by the sudden daylight. It was nearly midday. The trench was a picture of devastation. They stepped on corpses and the captain saw what the artillery bombardment had done to his positions. An earthquake had wrecked the trenches and only the dugout had withstood it.

"Duck!" said the lieutenant.

He ducked. A bullet ploughed up the dirt on the edge of the parapet. Red army soldiers stared at him as he passed. From a piece of even ground he saw the hill, a gigantic bald patch gleaming in the sun. Little columns of smoke hung over the ground. Perhaps their own shells, trying to seal off the Russian break-through. They made a wide circle. A couple of Red soldiers were carrying a wounded man. They were sweating and smelled of musk. The way to the front trenches had never seemed so long to the captain. The revolver which Trupikow held pointed at his back protected him from the hostility of the other soldiers. They came to the wrecked tank. On the side where it had been hit, the hole with its jagged steel edges looked like a shark's mouth gaping at him. A direct hit had fallen here. The sap broadened out into a roundel. In the middle of it lay a German soldier with his head sunk forward and his hands above his head. The captain bent down and saw the blackened, bloody hole of a bullet in his neck.

"Let's go on!" ordered the lieutenant angrily.

They reached the front line trench. Torn and ragged bodies in German uniform. Pools of dried blood. A distorted face without a body. The smashed machine-gun position. The gun itself had gone. Then more Red Army troops. They reached the furthest point at which they were still covered against the German fire. Near them a Russian machine gun was firing short bursts into the trench. Behind a low wall four Russians huddled close to each other, staring ahead.

"Here we are!" said Trupikow, throwing himself on the ground. "We are within hand grenade range here."

The captain sank down beside him in terror.

"All right, go ahead!" ordered Trupikow. He spat. A machine-gun bullet whistled away over his head.

"Hello! *Kameraden!*" called the captain.

"Louder!" urged Trupikow.

The captain put his hand to his mouth and shouted again: "Hello! *Kameraden!*"

A shaft with a black head sped through the air and landed with a thud in a puddle just in front of them. A moment later there came the detonation.

"Your men don't trust you," said Trupikow.

"It's your company commander," called the captain. "Do you understand me?" A hail of machine-gun bullets lashed through the air and churned up the earth. "Hello! Be sensible!" he called excitedly. "It's me, Captain Waldmüller!"

At last the firing ceased and an angry voice shouted: "Tommyrot, Comrade Ivan! We know you!" The captain tried to recognize this infuriated voice but he could not identify it. "Is that you, Lutz?" he asked.

"He's dead, you must have found his pay book!"

"No, it's me, Waldmüller!" he shouted in despair. "You must believe me."

There was a moment's silence and they seemed to be discussing things.

Then the voice called: "What's the name of our C.O.?"

"Major Schnitzer."

"And the runner?"

It was still the same voice which he could not recognize. "Braun!" he called.

"And what do you want of us?"

"I've been taken prisoner. I know what our situation is." The captain raised himself. "Your resistance is pointless. If you don't surrender. . . ." He looked at Trupikow who nodded. "You needn't be afraid. You will be treated decently."

He fell silent and waited for a moment.

"Captain!"

"Yes?"

"Why is our resistance pointless?"

"You're surrounded. The Russians are already in Emga." He looked around for the lieutenant's confirmation and noticed too late that it was not true. He began to sweat profusely.

"Wait!" came the voice from the other side. After a while someone asked: "Waldmüller, are you being threatened?"

Now he seemed to know the voice. Another sentence and he would recognize it.

"No," he called back.

"Waldmüller, don't talk nonsense. You're not speaking of your own free will."

The captain gave a start. He recognized the major's voice. How had he suddenly appeared in the trench? He must be in Podrowa. He looked helplessly at the Russian and stuttered: "I only want to avoid unnecessary bloodshed."

"Waldmüller!" called the major. "If you are being threatened we have a Russian captain here. I'm prepared to exchange the man for you."

"I'm not being forced," called the captain running his hand over his forehead. His hand was wet with sweat.

"Ask what his name is," whispered Trupikow.

"What's the name of the captain?"

"We don't know. He belongs to the outfit that has taken you prisoner."

"Sostschenko," murmured the lieutenant.

"The officer is wounded. Arrange an exchange. You for the Russian," called the major.

The captain was in despair. The peace he had had almost within his grasp was receding further and further. "Surrender!" ordered Trupikow angrily.

"The Russians don't accept your proposal," the captain called with relief. "It's completely futile. I advise you. ..."

"Waldmüller, I understand you. ..."

"Herr Major!" He no longer knew how he could convince him.

"Unbelievable," said the major. Then he asked point blank: "Tell me, Waldmüller, did you betray our dugout to the Russians?"

"Herr Major!" The captain suddenly remembered the sketch of the dugout and his hands began to tremble.

"Answer me!"

Lieutenant Trupikow looked with sudden interest at his revolver.

"Herr Major!" called the captain in despair. "Discuss the matter with your men."

"That's all, Waldmüller. I'm sorry for you. That's all!"

"Come with me," said the lieutenant with a smile. They were about to stand up when bullets began to whistle above their heads. They had to crawl back. German bullets, thought the captain. Would God never strike a bargain, then?

Chapter Nine

Sonja Schaljewa ran along a sunken road. The air stank of gunpowder. Charred grass was smoking on the embankment and in the deepest part of the gulley she saw the first dead man. He lay in the middle of the road and his bandaged arms were raised rigidly towards the sky. A truck had dropped him and none of the soldiers had paid any attention to him as they hurried past. She shivered in spite of her padded uniform, which was too thick for that warm morning.

Behind the parapet a railway line crossed the road. There were Red Army troops continuing in the same direction as herself, others coming from right or left and turning off along the track. She asked for information about the aid station to which she had been sent. A Commissar pointed to the railway track, turned around and hurried away.

She walked along the ties for some distance and asked a soldier the way to the hill. He replied that she was taking the shortest cut. Guns were firing from every direction in the woods. She increased her pace. A group of cossacks rode over the railway embankment. They shouted something incomprehensible and cracked their whips in the air. Runners hurried past and wounded men hobbled towards the rear. The earth trembled from the firing of the big guns, for a heavy barrage was being laid on the German front line.

Gradually the distance between the sleepers became too wide for her steps. She had to pick her way over the sharp gravel. Her feet began to burn. The railway track seemed to have no end but at last she reached a clearing— a green meadow pitted with black shell holes. The log hut which had been described to her was being used as a first-aid post. Red Army soldiers with white bandages stood all around it. Some of them lay apathetically in the grass. Others were groaning. She saw grey haggard faces and mud-stained uniforms. The sweat ran down her face and her hair hung down in strands on her forehead. She staggered painfully over to the hut for she could not take a rest now. Her first question as she recognized one of the Siberians was: "Have you seen Captain Sostschenko?"

"No." The man lay in the grass and his face was turned up toward the sky. Blood was running from his lips.

"Is there any one from Sostschenko's battalion here?" she cried.

Six men replied.

"Have you seen the captain?"

"If you could give us some water, comrade."

"Have you seen the captain?"

"No."

"No. . . . No. . . . I think. . . ."

She was ashamed of her question and made her way into the hut. Perhaps once inside she would learn something.

As soon as she opened the door she found herself staring into a slaughterhouse. She thought she would suffocate and was incapable of any movement. A doctor with a bloodstained apron came over to her.

"Comrade, I've been waiting an hour for you. At last a woman's hand." He put an apron into her hands.

"Have you any news of Captain Sostschenko?" she asked in a dull voice.

"Please don't make things difficult, comrade. I need you urgently." He fastened the apron around her waist.

She saw a table with an oil cloth top, and instruments glittering in a pail.

"Next!" He did not even give her time to look around. Rough hands lifted a body onto a table.

"I would be satisfied even if you would just hold their hands," said the doctor. "A woman can work wonders with them."

She caught hold of the wounded man's hand. He had a bloodstained bandage on his head. A stretcher bearer peeled it off as though the skull were a fruit. The congealed blood tore like paper. She was standing at the upper end of the table and now before her eyes was a white, pulsating mass.

"Can you see the splinter?" asked the doctor.

She could see nothing but blood on the man's forehead. A silver needle bored into the jelly of the brain. It bubbled and then collapsed. She had an overwhelming desire to vomit.

"I've got it," said a voice in the far distance. She closed her eyes. "That's it!"

When she looked up again the stretcher bearer was already busy with a new bandage. She wanted to implore them to let her go, but she could not utter a sound. The room began to spin. She planted her feet wide apart.

"Next!"

The next man had lost both hands.

"Hold his head!" ordered the doctor.

This time she shut her eyes immediately. She tried to picture Sostschenko. The stable lamp smoked. The horse snorted. "He's done for!" said the doctor. She opened her eyes in terror.

"He's dead!" said the doctor impatiently to the orderly. The wounded man was no longer breathing.

"Next!"

"Are you wounded?" asked the doctor.

"I'm sick."

"Sick?"

"He hasn't even got a temperature," said the orderly.

"Is he feverish, comrade?"

She put her hand on the soldier's forehead. He is feverish, she thought, and so am I. We're all feverish. The soldier was still young and she looked into his eyes. "You must go back to the company," she said. "Back to Captain Sostschenko. He needs every man now."

"Yes, comrade." The soldier turned away and staggered out of the hut like a drunken man.

"Next!" said the doctor wearily.

She wanted to change places. From the other side she could have looked out of the window. But it was impossible. The floor was covered with wounded men and only the side where she stood was free. She looked at the white oilcloth. The soldier on the table had a small, impudent mustache and was drunk.

"I can't feel anything," he boasted.

The orderly pulled down his bloodstained trousers, looked in terror at his superior and then at her.

"Bandage him quickly!" said the doctor.

"What is it?" asked the wounded man. Before she could prevent it he had raised himself on his elbows. An animal cry came from his lips as he saw the wound. He beat his feet on the table. He raged, screamed and wept. His saliva bubbled. Then suddenly he collapsed and his features relaxed. He had grown old in a matter of seconds. The mustache seemed to be a theatrical prop. He would never be able to court a woman again. He let himself be bandaged and carried out without a murmur.

"Next!"

They laid him down like a board on the table. He lay in a canvas sheet. His body under the covering only reached down to the upper thigh. The orderly put the pail with the instruments where his feet should have been.

When Sonja realized what they were going to do with him she looked away. Again her thoughts returned to

Sostschenko and the little attic room in Leningrad. He sat next to her stroking her hand. She could feel his tenderness almost physically. A bitter melancholy took hold of her. They would never again be together like that. Life lay ahead of her like a disconsolate road which ends in a rubbish heap. . . . A shell burst on the nearby meadow making the instruments rattle in the pail. There was a sound of sawing.

"The other one, too," said the doctor.

A second explosion made the earth shake and the roof beams rattle. Smoke seeped through the open window and the saw went on scraping as if there were nothing except this hut, except men who had too many bones.

With the next shells they heard the firing explosions. Two, three, four, furious detonations shook the house. The door was ripped out of its frame and the smoke swirled in. The soldiers outside poured into the hut like animals in search of shelter.

"Quiet!" ordered the doctor, without stopping his work. From outside, a cat jumped in on the window sill. Its back was arched. It wanted to be near people.

"Is his pulse still beating, comrade?"

She could feel nothing, only cold bony hands. A ring hung loose on one of the thin fingers. More and more soldiers pressed into the room pushing each other, jostling around the table, stepping on the wounded men on the floor. All of them were looking for protection under a roof that could no longer give protection.

"Stay outside, you idiots!" roared the orderly.

A deafening explosion and the room was flooded with a harsh light. The orderly fell to the ground and the noise of the saw fell silent.

"Comrade!"

She only saw that they all ducked. The cat sprang over the bodies onto the table. Dust swirled through the air and came to rest on the white oil cloth, on her lips, on the instruments in the pail.

"Help the sergeant, comrade!"

She let go of the ice-cold hands and bent down to the pail. Another burst and the table collapsed. Screams. Her hands clawed the air. Her feet stepped on bodies, on faces. She rushed out. The grass under her feet was like a fleece. The meadow was indescribably green. She fell down beneath the first tree and wept. Perhaps for Sostschenko. She felt that he had abandoned her. She wept for herself because she loved him.

Chapter Ten

Mortar shells had been bursting for half an hour in the trench by the foxhole and on the dugout of the surrounded Schnitzer group. They came from the sap occupied by the Reds in front of company headquarters, somersaulted in the air like steel beer bottles and exploded with unpleasant accuracy just in front of the entrance. No corner was safe. The depth of the trench was no help now and they all crouched in the trap. It seemed incredible that the Russians had spotted this dugout for the trench could not be seen, and there were no dead men on the parapet. A fiendish luck seemed to guide the mortar shells and Major Schnitzer was convinced that the name of this luck was Captain Waldmüller. Actually it was the fault of the Russian hand grenades, which had fallen not in the captain's dugout but over the wall of the trench. In any case the luck was quite methodical. It snuffed out Corporal Schute as a puff of wind would have snuffed out a candle.

The runner left the corporal lying where he was and barricaded the dugout. A chink remained open so that he could still see a part of the trench. He snuggled down in the entrance leading to the foxhole and peered out.

The foxhole gave evidence that the key position had seen better days. On the night the shock troop engineers had relieved the infantry company they had found proof of it. A signboard with the words Villa Foxhole. *Had it still been in its original spot it would have been almost a sign of peace and security. The way in which it was found, however, proved the opposite. The sappers had maintained that the trench was not deep enough. They immediately began to build a parapet and realized at once that the maze of trenches in this key position had served at the same time as a mass burial ground. Four or five inches under the ground they came upon corpses. Their spades cut through rotting flesh and banged against bones and splintered limbs. By the light of the flares they came across a skull still wearing a Russian steel helmet and a skeleton held together by a moldy belt. Thousands of little flies swarmed in the trench. Poisonous fumes flew into the faces of those who had no gas masks. The key position had become a plague pit. Like men possessed, grotesque shadows shovelled the rubbish over the parapet. They looked like divers in a sunken ship staring at each other through their round helmet windows. The mass grave had three layers. The diggers had to put on gloves when they could not work with shovels. And between these layers they found the rotting piece of wood with the inscription:* Villa Foxhole. *It must have been painted by one of the bony hands which had now been shovelled over the parapet. Here there had been a time when, stripped to the waist, men had leaned against the trench wall, smoked cigarettes, spoken of leave,*

*and lit a fire to keep off the mosquitoes. But that was a
long time ago.*

The corridor in which the runner now lay was like a fun-
nel which led obliquely into the earth. Narrow as a drain
pipe, damp and dark. At the end was an entrance with a
stout wooden door. A big crate-lid with leather hasps and
the inscription: "Army Property—Fragile." Behind this
door was an anteroom, an inexplicable luxury. Perhaps it
was an antigas chamber. It was too narrow for people to
live in but it had been lined with duck boards and plastered
with old newspapers. Anyone who was bored could read
that the German armies in the east were advancing, that
Herr Maier had passed away peacefully and that on Mon-
day there would be another distribution of eggs. But that
must have been a hundred years ago. Behind the anteroom
was a second crate lid leading to the living quarters. There
was plenty of room for a whole squad, but the ceiling was
too low for the men to stand up. On the floor was something
that must once have been hay. Clay-covered boots and
foul air had changed it into a rotting manure. On this manure lay nine wounded men, including Captain Sostschenko.
Early that morning there had been eleven, but the runner
had dragged two of them out and rolled them over the parapet. They had bled to death. From this room an opening,
hung with a canvas sheet, led to the sleeping quarters. A
direct hit had laid it waste. The shell had caught Russian
soldiers in their sleep. They had tried in vain to take the
bodies out, but the debris could not be cleared or the foxhole would have collapsed. No, they had had no illusions

about the place from the very beginning. Nor did the captain, who was now a Russian prisoner in the company headquarters dugout. Nor the sergeant major who had deserted to Emga. Nor the sergeant who was still firing the machine gun, and certainly not he, the runner. The dugout was like a dark tomb and smelled like an animal's lair.

Therefore, and for another reason as well, the runner had lain down in the corridor. When a mortar burst outside the entrance he quickly turned his head aside. This was far better than lying down at the bottom of the hole and having to put up with the groaning of the wounded men. In front of the entrance the dead Corporal Schute was being hit again and again by shrapnel splinters. Because of this he kept moving and looked as though he were still alive, or had St. Vitus' dance. Once he waved his hand, and another time he turned around and his lifeless eyes stared at the runner as though they were saying: "Well, what have you got to say to this?" And there wasn't much one could say. . . .

The swimming pool in Schute's garden would never be built now. Unless Frau Schute decided to marry again. She looked fairly young on the picture the corporal had shown him. A letter from her was still in the dead man's breast pocket. It was only a week old and had already been torn by a splinter. Actually it was quite a harmless letter: he shouldn't worry about her. Everything was all right. Then a little news about the garden, and about a servant girl (now it was impossible to find one) and about a room which could not be allowed to remain empty. The tenant was very pleasant. And further: one heard so much about soldiers who got entangled with girls. She was broadminded—life was short. An understanding wife, Frau Schute. A modern outlook—perhaps a little too modern. Various things in the letter were not particularly clear to the recipient and the runner had to read it too. He pretended not to understand it either. But he had seen another letter about which Schute knew nothing. "Read it," the battalion adjutant had said to him, "and then decide whether the letter should be given to Schute or not." It was from a neighbor telling how people gossiped about Frau Schute's relationship with the tenant. It was a very explicit letter. The runner looked at the adjutant and shook his head. According to the laws of probability the problem would solve itself. The calculation had been correct. For a short time there would be mourning for the sake of appearances, silent handshakes, grave faces. The tenant would still be pleasant. Life is short. Had Schute himself not also. . . . No? His fault then, considering that his wife was so broadminded. There were girls everywhere. A soldier's life is a gay one. Big fireworks on Hill 308. Shock troops, raid against the Russian bunker position. Corporal Schute, out on the right flank. Green flares. Artillery attack. Machine-gun bursts. A two-hundred-yard sprint across open country. Hand grenades. Life is short, soldier. Naturally a stranger in the house is cause for gossip. Mine laying at midnight. Schute with the safety catch off. Russian machine guns spraying no man's land. Every spot of cover to be used. With a live mine your life hangs on a thin thread. You can be certain that I'm broad-

*minded. At 0610: the attack. Weapons loaded. Forward,
Schute, out of your trench. The heart throbs in the throat
and the lungs are ready to burst. Press on under cover of
the barrage. Barbed wire. Take out the pins. Alert in the
grey dawn. Reds in front of the trench. Hand grenades out.
Too late! They're already jumping in. Take your rifle butt,
bayonet, spade. You must kill. For your wife, Schute.
For a . . .*

The runner took a stone and flung it at dead Corporal
Schute's face. He wanted to go back in the foxhole below
and look once more at the perspiring scarecrow with the
protruding teeth and the wound in the hip. Backwards on
all fours, he slipped down into the corridor. He slid on the
damp earth, kicked the crate-lid door open, and groped in
the dark along the newspaper wall. At last he found the
door to the living quarters. In front of him in the dim candlelight lay a groaning bundle—the replacement with a
face like a horse and the torn-open hip, the baker. Red-
rimmed eyes stared at him.

"So your story was true?" growled the runner angrily.
"You slept with soldiers' wives and paid them in bread.
You presented the colonel in the recruiting office with a
car. You bribed the burgomaster with money. You and
your mill! But it didn't do you any good." The horse-faced
youth looked at him in consternation. "You spilled the
beans while you were feverish, you pig!" shrieked the runner, triumphantly. "Now it's caught up with you. We're
surrounded. And you'll never get out of this shit hole again."

He spat at the wall and staggered out. He was oblivious

to the wail of the wounded, to the mortars which at any moment might blow him to pieces. He did not see the bursts, not even dead Schute. He took his rifle and broke off the butt, threw the broken weapon into the foxhole and climbed up onto the trench wall. Before he got to his feet he took the crumpled pass out of his pocket. Then he leapt out and ran at full speed with his arms raised, holding the scrap of paper in his right hand.

The Russian fire suddenly ceased, and now all around him the silence was deathlike. All he could hear was his own breathing and the splashing noise of his feet when he stepped in a puddle. Each moment he waited for the whip-lash sound of bullets behind or in front of him. But nothing happened. His boots grew heavier. Each step brought him nearer to the strip of marsh. He had forgotten that. The mud clung to his feet like lead. "I must get through," he thought in despair. The images before his eyes merged one into the other. Mad visions began to dance in front of him: the high ground, his two children stretching out their hands to him and finally two fire balls. His feet sank ankle deep in the peaty slime. A few yards further on it came up to his calves. He lost one boot and then another. Now he hurried forward barefoot, waving the pink scrap of paper like a maniac. The bandage on his thumb worked lose and fluttered above his head like a white flag.

And at last he reached the barbed wire. His uniform was in tatters. Scratches and aching limbs. Dead Russians were hanging in the barbed wire. Tortured faces under battered helmets. Now. . . .

Now the shot must come. From over there, or from behind. But it did not come. Nobody seemed to notice him. Or were they all staring at him? Did they watch his cowardice and not consider him worth a bullet? The sergeant's voice: "You coward!" His own voice: "I'm not a coward!" "A deserter!" mocked the sergeant. But no one had called to him. A ghost had been mocking him. The barbed wire now lay behind him and he fell exhausted into a hollow. Jittery with fear he waved the pink leaflet in front of a face with a pair of slit eyes.

Two and then three brown figures flung themselves on him, pressed his arms to the ground and went through his pockets. They let him loose. An unmistakable jerk of the hand made him understand that he should go on crawling along the hollow. A guard remained behind him. Overhead, the hissing of bullets from the German trenches. At last he dared to stand up. The squat tube of a trench mortar pointed to the sky. Hostile faces stared at him. On the flat terrain a tank with the gun pointed westward. Men were crouching under cover of the tank walls. No one looked at the scrap of paper which the runner still held in his hand although he waved it at almost everyone.

A figure in a leather uniform climbed out of the tank and jumped down beside him in the hollow. The commissar carried his revolver on a cord around his neck. He came up to him and hit him a hard blow in the face. The blow burnt on his cheek and he felt sick. He began to pant and his bare feet hurt him. Once more he tried the effect of the leaflet but the commissar tore it out of his hand and stamped on it. Now, he thought, I've lost the most important thing of all. The commissar screamed at him but he could not understand a word. More blows. Brutal hands ripped open his pockets; the picture of his children, the snapshot of his wife—torn and flung into the mud. The runner began to weep. The commissar spat in his face, and shouted an order. One of the Red soldiers caught the runner by the arm and dragged him away. He was kicked from behind and another blow fell on his head. He fell to the ground. His hands groped for a piece of the photograph. He tumbled into a trench behind his guard.

The trench led to the rear. They stumbled over dead Russians. One of them reminded him of Corporal Schute, and all at once they seemed to him familiar faces, white and lifeless as in a wax figure cabinet. Their skin reminded him of velvety peaches. The lips seemed to move and he saw a mocking grin.

"Leave me alone!" he roared. His companion hit him in the chest with his rifle butt. The last word became a gurgle. He staggered on. They reached the slope, which led up steeply to the west. Countless shell craters almost lip to lip and the runner was thrust into one of them. A squad of Red soldiers took over and led him into a subterranean corridor from whose roof the water dripped. Just like the foxhole, thought the runner, but wider and damper. They reached a cave. He saw a wobbly table and the interrogation began. He stood in a puddle of water, barefoot. A candle dripped onto the table. He was ready to drop, and the cold rose up his legs. A soft voice behind the candle asked him questions. He could not make out the face for he could not see through the flickering flame. Behind it everything was in darkness. He did not dare to move. Near his own face a hand toyed with a revolver. When he would not answer the first question he felt the cold barrel in his neck. The voice asked question after question. He had to reply quickly and resolutely. When he hesitated the revolver butt came down on the back of his head. His skull felt as though it would burst. He did not know where he found the answers. They flew at him. What company: What battalion? The name of your commanding officer? How strong is your unit? Where is the artillery? He answered every question. He wanted to interrupt and tell them that he had deserted. On the leaflet he had read that he would be treated decently. The voice gave him no time. An inhuman machine sat opposite him. The icy cold of the puddle had risen to his loins. His head was burning and his thumb began to hurt. He tottered. The candle flame seemed to be wobbling to and fro. But they knew no pity. He answered in broken phrases. They beat him, stamped on his stomach. His knees were bleeding and he ran his tongue over his gums. His teeth lay in bleeding stumps on the floor. They kicked his testicles until he collapsed. As he fell he tried to beg for mercy but his voice would not respond. He tried with gestures to explain that he was a deserter. They dragged him outside and pushed him down the steep slope. He rolled over and over and his battered face fell in earth. He hit his forehead against a stone. When he opened his eyes he saw a new torturer. He no longer felt the blows with which they forced him to his feet and propelled him forward. He staggered through the hollow, past guns, piles of ammunition, Red troops. They looked at him as though he had come from the underworld. He spat blood. His tattered trousers now covered only his loins. Bits of uniform cloth stuck to his dirty and bloodstained thighs. His legs swayed like steel whips; they were now mere bones and sinews. He moved in the sunlight and his shadow hopped behind him like a malicious imp. He looked like a shy cave creature that had wandered by mistake into the daylight and, blinded by the sun, was looking for some corner into which to creep.

He would have stumbled over a stretcher had his guard not caught his arm. The Red soldier made him pick up the stretcher. He could see only the back of the other bearer—a Russian. They had to carry a wounded man. His guard could not drive him any more, but now the weight of the stretcher threatened to pull him down. He was as stiff as a rod. At each step he felt a jab in the spine, at each uneven patch of ground a burning pain in his chest. He clenched his smashed jaws. He had to cough. He spat. A bloody clot of phlegm fell in the grass.

The wounded man on the stretcher stared at him. He was afraid that this battered bundle of a man would let him drop. With glassy eyes the runner saw the eyes turned on him full of hatred. Strange noises began to buzz in his ears like a hammer beating against tree trunks. A blast swept him aside and he saw the guns with their quivering muzzles raised to the sky. He heard nothing more; he was deaf.

When he arrived at the crowded first aid station he was allowed to put down the stretcher. He was hustled to and fro. Soldiers pushed him out of the way—Red Army soldiers, filthy and wearing tattered uniforms like his own. His guard was swallowed up in the crowd. Strange noises came through his ear drums as in a fog. A white apron appeared. Two hands carefully took off his tunic. A needle was plunged into his right arm and immediately a sweet stream of warmth and well-being ran through him. The drumming disappeared in the back of his head and his muscles relaxed. He sank to the ground in exhaustion. Like an onlooker he noted that someone touched him, bound up his thumb, rubbed a smarting fluid on his gums with a finger. He was given a place in the grass. An overcoat that smelt of camphor was pulled over him and he sank into an ocean of oblivion. In the noisy turmoil of the aid station he thought that he had found the best spot on this earth.

Chapter Eleven

THE FLOOD poured out of the forest from Podrowa, whirled past the walls of the barn and surged against the depot at Emga. It came from the low-lying country behind the hill, out of the marshes, from the crossroads, from every point where, in the grey morning light, positions had still been intact east of Emga. As in the case of every panic the initial cause was insignificant: a column of tanks advancing slowly along the Podrowa log road in the direction of Emga. The olive green crates had to follow each other along the narrow road. The machine gun of the leading tank drove hundreds of soldiers before it and swept along all who were trying to preserve discipline and order—the able-bodied, the wounded, officers and men. Gunners left their loaded guns. Fresh replacements threw their weapons away. The stampeding mass of soldiers, like a herd of cattle, absorbed them. New groups were spewed out of the marsh to right and left of the highway. An officer who opposed them was flung ruthlessly into the morass. When he had freed himself from the sticky mud the human tide had already trampled past. All that remained were the last ranks in which death reaped a rich harvest. Here hobbled the wounded and the weak ones. The machine guns mowed them down like scythes. And, like a lizard, the column always grew a new tail.

Towards midday they reached Emga and swarmed on to the station. They rushed senselessly at a train without an engine. Hundreds fought for a place in carriages which were not even coupled together. Whoever found a place defended it as if his life were at stake. Rifle butts banged down on hands that tried to catch hold of the iron handles. Kicks and blows. Brutal fists hammered on heads until they toppled backwards. Terrified faces, imploring hands, wounds that had re-opened. Hate and hostility. Fights for standing room in carriages with dismantled wheels. Between the rails teemed the stragglers, the desperate, men with amputated limbs and in high fever, men who had lost their hands and could not clutch at anything. The goal for everyone was the train. The train that was no train. The *fata morgana* on the dead rails. Carriages without buffers. Wheels that could no longer turn.

The car on its way to Emga only made contact with the fringe of this turmoil. The judge advocate next to the driver stared the panic boldly in the face. Troop movements were of no interest to him. Undisciplined units, he thought. He was only interested in legal problems.

Not until he came to the town square did his driver have any difficulties. The car was hemmed in. The colonel had to get out and push his way through the soldiers to reach the commandant's headquarters. The physical proximity of unwashed soldiers made him feel sick. With half-closed eyes he let himself be carried by the stream towards the building. He had his orders to thank for this unpleasant episode: "The judge advocate is to set up an immediate court-martial of a deserter in Emga. The enforcement of the sentence is to be reported forthwith to G.H.Q." It was a very vague order. A deserter in Emga. Which one? The enforcement of the sentence. What sentence? Such a thing demanded preparation, reports, sessions. The colonel, who in civilian life was a state's attorney, worked by paragraphs. Legal paragraphs were always made up of lucid, unadorned sentences with subjects and predicates. In the army order, the heart of the matter seemed to lie between the lines. Namely: that extraordinary conditions demand extraordinary measures. That, at least, was how it appeared to him. He shivered like a conscientious bookkeeper when a draft blows through his office door. This was out of his province. He stuck closely to precedent. For him, inferences were thin ice. Also, in the order it said that he was left responsible for the sentencing. That, in any case, was according to the regulations. He had made up his mind that he must obey, and in the event of difficulties he could always cite this. What was between the lines was no affair of his.

In the turmoil of this flood the commandant's headquarters was the lifeboat. It was the meeting place for everyone with a bad conscience who had already abandoned the sinking ship. Everyone tried to cover up his failure with some demand. But the regional commandant, a short tubby major, had nothing to give except blank forms. He ran around with a flushed face and heavy responsibilities. He listened to every possible request and in fact heard nothing. "My battery needs ammunition at once. Otherwise I cannot be responsible." The guns of this battery were standing deserted by the highway. The gunners were defending their seats in the ghost train. It was common knowledge that the commandant had no ammunition at his disposal. "If my detachment does not get any gas I must blow up my trucks." The trucks were there only on paper. They stood burning in the forest, loaded with equipment and a gas reserve for three days. The officer commanding the detachment had himself set fire to one of them. "At least give me a vehicle for the main aid station. I must get my men away." The staff doctor's car was stuck in the swamp. He needed the vehicle urgently for himself. "I want written confirmation that my battalion is unfit for action.... I need medical supplies.... I need cartridges.... I need replacements urgently. . . . Sorry, without antitank weapons it's impossible. . . . I refuse all responsibility . . . refuse all responsibility . . . refuse responsibility." The major, who half an hour ago had been named combat commander at Emga, had already heard this sentence a hundred times. In addition to this there was the noise outside the window, the whine of Russian fighter planes, the thunder of the antiaircraft shells and the ringing of the telephones. Luftwaffe ground station: "Where is the front line?" Army Corps: "Emergency powers for the combat commander at Emga." Quartermaster: "You are responsible for all the provisions." Division: "Request report on the situation." Those idiots!

The judge advocate, with the rank of colonel, had to run after the major who was sprinting through the rooms like a weasel. The atmosphere here was a familiar one to him. When they recognized him—and all of them recognized him—came the cold mouthing of his title which he took for respect. He should have felt at home: insecurity, nervous expectation, sideway glances—exactly as it was when he entered the hall of the Law Courts. State's attorney swathed in robe and dignity, striding forward, confident of his paragraphs. The servile greetings were a means of self preservation.

They all saluted him. To his delight he realized that they almost bowed. Only the M.P. sergeant stood there stiff as a ramrod. An attempt on the part of this representative of the law to deflect a little of the general respect towards himself. In any case, order reigned here. Perhaps things weren't so bad outside after all. Still—extraordinary circumstances; that was why he was here. At last he caught up with the major and said: "In view of my orders will you please give me the facilities to enable me to start my inquiry." Actually he could have given a direct order for the Army stood behind him, but he never forgot to be polite among his peers.

The major who was not up to the occasion suddenly decided to take it as a joke. "I'll put all the officers here at your disposal." He looked at the colonel as a clown looks at his own reflection in a mirror, waiting for the smile that must come. For some strange reason the smile never came.

"Are the gentlemen all unemployed then?" came the surprised question.

"Of course." Even a battle commander is entitled to a little grim humor. If this clown from the army wanted a circus put on, all right. The term, "battle commander," rose in the major's nose like laughing gas. It couldn't matter less, he thought with a gurgle of pleasure. Let all the deserters that have collected here court-martial the absent ones. He felt like a hero in underpants. "Take whomever you want," he said generously. He could not help laughing. His adjutant stood behind him: "Division is on the line."

The timing was perfect. The major vanished before the colonel could ask for explanations.

The colonel looked around the room. He had always loathed slovenliness. In order to feel at ease he had to create a certain setting for himself. The table there, in the middle of the room. Take away those boxes. Some sweeping would not hurt. Too bad that the officers did not rush for their brooms. He chose two from among the bystanders. The remainder vanished into thin air. The room was suddenly empty.

"What is the meaning of all that hubbub outside?" he asked. "I had to fight my way through. No one paid any attention to my rank."

"The retreat, colonel!" Now they knew that he was an

idiot and they smiled sourly. This was the last straw. The ground was burning under their feet. But they must be careful; this man was dangerous.

He definitely gave the impression that he was not afraid. They exchanged meaningful glances. In fact, none of them knew what he wanted of them. A deserter? There were thousands of them here! Either the army order was already three days old or the bastard was hiding something from them.

The colonel was hiding nothing from them. An order was an order even if it were couched ambiguously. With his arrival at the regional commander's office the official proceedings had begun. He understood how to handle a court martial. Now everything would proceed according to plan. First the rules and procedures. He was like an old maid who, oblivious to the present, pores over faded love letters. This rummaging in his brief case, the opening of his law books—even the smell of damp here reminded him of the smell in the court room.

"The list of prisoners, please," he said, turning to the M.P. sergeant who was hovering near him like a well-trained bloodhound. His bureaucratic mannerisms drove the two officers to distraction.

The cavalry captain had left his vehicle standing outside the commander's headquarters. He had come to create an alibi for himself. From the window he watched his driver fidgeting at the steering wheel. He was getting impatient and at any moment would drive off without him. Surreptitiously he tried to attract his attention but the questioning glance of the colonel nailed him to the spot and his gesture became a casual wave out of the window.

The colonel thought that these were not the most dignified colleagues he'd ever had. "May I have your names, gentlemen?" They stammered like schoolboys. Now they were stuck. Their hopes of slipping away died. Each of them feverishly tried to think of a way out. The hammer of the heavy machine gun outside spurred them on but each idea foundered against the colonel's calm. He was studying the charge sheet of the soldier against whose name stood the word "Desertion." He seemed to remember the case. The preliminary investigation was already closed and it would not take long to conclude the case. He vaguely remembered a childlike, half-starved figure. In the preliminary investigation he had been under the impression that the boy had already given up hope for himself. The only excuse he proffered was that he had done it for his mother. Compassion? There was no mention of it in the regulations.

"Bring him in!" ordered the colonel. The M.P. sergeant went out and the colonel began to swear in his colleagues. They looked at his face. Behind the pince-nez stuck on his red-veined nose his eyes seemed to be set too close together. He raised his hand and exhorted both officers, irrespective of personal feelings, to see that justice was carried out. He himself would act as President of the court-martial and also conduct the prosecution. The cavalry captain whose car was waiting outside would play the part of the defense counsel. The other officer had merely to act as a witness. The men listened with bowed heads. The empty room reminded them of an execution platform.

Shot rangs out in Emga. Either the Russians had already arrived or the military police were getting trigger happy.

The colonel went on reading as if he were reciting scripture. The defense was to confine itself to the facts. Unless there were good reasons for it, there should be no intervention. The witness should see that the regulations were followed. At the end he would have to testify to the orderly conduct of the court-martial. He himself would pronounce judgment. He thought it might be the detention barracks. Moreover he wanted to make it short. Both officers exchanged glances: Who would still believe that!

The driver outside the window had spotted his battery commander and was tapping on the broken window.

"Tell him to go to the devil," said the colonel. The cavalry captain could manage only a rather vague wave of the hand. The driver was not going to be put off. He paced up and down outside the window. He had known his chief long enough to suspect that higher authority was at work here. His behavior was rather like that of a policeman patrolling the street outside a cheap restaurant. Each time he passed he glanced through the window.

The colonel began to get annoyed.

"What does that man want?" he asked.

"I don't know him," lied the captain. In the dusky room no one noticed that he had turned scarlet. At last the sergeant brought in the victim.

The members of the court were shocked. If he deserved any punishment he had already paid the price. The eyes of this boy with the sloping shoulders looked right through them. They seemed to know everything. The cavalry captain thought of his own burning trucks. He had given the order to set fire to them and that was enough to finish his career. At least thirty men of his company had heard him. He saw their eyes open wide and read the terror in them. Yet he had only done what they had all wanted. His order had released them from the fetters of discipline; like madmen they had set fire to the bales of straw and had scattered to the four winds. Any one who wanted to settle an old score—and even in his company there were old scores to be settled—had only to come forward and tell the story. Then he too would be in the soup. The representative of justice standing there in front of him adored such cases. He knew nothing of fear, nothing of certain degradations. The most wretched life is a gift full of exciting moments. Where will one find a man foolish enough to fling it away? At such moments one has longings; for a slice of bread, for a prayer, for a drink of water. The young prisoner looked straight through him. Perhaps the prisoner company would not be the worst thing for him. If God willed it he would survive that too. . . .

The colonel opened the proceedings. "We have enough evidence," he said pompously, "but for the sake of order tell us once more what happened. That dawn when the attack began you were not to be found. Why?"

Had he himself ever lain behind a parapet waiting for

the signal he would never have put the question. Perhaps the opportunity was favorable and the man next to him was out of sight. Things should have gone off all right but something intervened. When he heard his name being called it was too late. In this second he might have run in utter despair with the others through the hail of bullets. An attack of mad bravery might have made a hero of him. Too late. An agent of fate flung him into the abyss. The cold face with the pince-nez was the agent and fate combined. The ears which belonged to this face would be deaf to the breaking of his bones.

Rifle fire racked Emga. The colonel seemed to take it for target practice. If the youngster had any sense he would prolong the trial until the Russians came. Almost unconsciously the cavalry captain looked out of the window. His driver had started up the car. He felt like drawing his revolver but he did not know whom he should shoot—the colonel, the fleeing driver or the childish bag of bones who was the cause of it all.

"Hold on a minute!" said the cavalry captain, rushing out of the room before the colonel could say a word.

The captain reached the courtyard. The driver and car had gone and the road was deserted in the bright midday sun. A few wounded men were hobbling towards the station. A machine gun was rattling at the exit to the village. Slowly, as though he had only wanted a breath of fresh air, he turned around and went back into the building. He hurried along the corridor with the whitewashed walls, past tin boxes full of papers and legal documents. For a moment, he had to lean against an oven which had been built into the wall. When he reentered the courtroom the colonel barely took notice of his returning. In a loud cynical voice he was addressing the boy: "Do you know what you are? A disgrace to your mother." Then followed a flood of abuse and cutting mockery. The soldier's face darkened. He murmured incoherent words and raised his hands in entreaty. The deep set eyes turned to the other members of the court. "Your mother will be ashamed of you," went on the colonel. "You coward!"

The cavalry captain felt the word like a stab.

"Tell him what he has deserved," said the colonel turning to the two officers. "Tell him," he repeated since there was no reply. They lowered their eyes. The contemptible performance made them sick.

"Let him go free," said the cavalry captain impulsively. He did not know how he mustered the courage to say this.

The colonel's face contorted. "Is that the reply of an officer?" He seemed to be looking around for a weapon to chastise this man who had contradicted him. "I shall pronounce judgment." His voice became calm, cool and impersonal. A cold glance at the young prisoner. The other members of the court martial heard only the end of the phrase: ". . . to death by shooting." They sat there frozen to stone as though the judgment had been pronounced upon them. The boy stood there without moving. The sergeant tapped his fingers nervously. "And you will carry out the sentence," went on the colonel, pointing to the cavalry captain, "and you will do it forthwith." The captain turned pale. "Me?"

"Yes, you. Behind the courthouse. Wherever you like. There's plenty of space." The colonel behaved as if the condemned man were no longer in the room. "You have a pistol, haven't you?" he asked casually.

"I object!"

"Overruled!" The colonel looked around. He had forgotten that there was no public here. He gathered up his papers. He nodded to the sergeant. There was a pause. The colonel was standing behind the table. Like a bored spectator he turned to the window. A distant rattle of a machine gun. The window pane tinkled. A hole appeared in the glass. A slight hiss. The colonel put his hands up to his face and then let them fall. They were red with blood. The officers saw a battered face, bloodflecked eyes in a bloody mask. The pince-nez lay broken on the table. The colonel slumped like a sack on his chair and there was a rattle in his throat. Mucus dripped from his nostrils. The bullet had shot away his lower jaw. Never again would he be able to pronounce a sentence.

The cavalry captain let him fall unaided to the ground. Only the sergeant M.P. leaped briskly to his aid. The young soldier still stood there as if nailed to the spot. The machine gun kept rattling at the exit to the village.

The regional commander appeared in the door with two soldiers.

"A stray bullet," said the captain.

The fat major shook his head. "Carry him outside," he ordered the soldiers. The sergeant opened the door smartly. "What about the sentence?" asked the major. He looked at the young prisoner. "That's not the right fellow," he said angrily. "I knew right away that judge advocate was a bloody fool. If the Army wants to make an example of someone you don't choose an ordinary enlisted man."

"If you don't do things yourself!" he went on, grumbling. "Half an hour ago I reported to headquarters that a sergeant major was being shot. A warning to others; the news will be circulated throughout the army. And this fool wastes his time with the wrong man." He raised his hand angrily: "Clear out!" he shouted to the boy who staggered from the room as though he had just awakened from a dream. "Get out!" he shouted to the M.P. sergeant. When they were left alone he looked at the captain. "The worst is over," he said. "Fresh troops have occupied the fringe of the sector. I hope they can hold it." He wriggled his stomach and was about to leave but turned once more to the captain. "You must shoot the sergeant major, unobtrusively," he said quietly.

A spider's web in the doorway swayed gently in the draft. The firing at the exit to the village grew louder. Two tanks rattled past the window. On the square outside, a company of infantry lined up in battle order.

Chapter Twelve

Sostschenko was in agony with his hip. The foxhole was like a grave. Through glazed eyes he could see a candle and dark shadows on the walls. Shadows all around him. His skin was on fire with fever. When he asked for water he received no reply. One of the enemy soldiers handed him a mess cup containing a few drops of fiery liquid. He listened to his breathing: there was a rattle in his throat. All the wounded men had rattles in their throats. Air, air! The grave must eventually open. He turned over on his side but this did not help.

"Tovarich?" he called in the dark. No reply. The enemy soldiers did not understand. The light grew dimmer and the shadows on the walls began to creep towards him. The sweat beaded on his forehead. He plunged his hands into the filth on which he lay and kneaded the bloody mess because it was cool. This lightened the pain. His hands dug deeper, dug into the damp earth. He rubbed his wet fingers over his lips. Gently he stroked his wound; his hip had gone numb. Near him was a shadow that did not sweat. He encountered a limp hand in the mud. Put it to his forehead. The hand did not move. It was cold. Suddenly he flung it back in horror. His fever rose. The grave was warm. He would have preferred it cold. The light was dim. He wanted it bright. A rattle in the throat. The shadows in the abyss rattled in harmony. A hot flush ran through him, enveloped him. The candles guttered. He felt moisture on his lips and in his throat. He thought he could hear his hot gums hissing. A hand stroked his forehead.

"Have we taken the hill?" he asked.

The German soldier did not understand him. . . .

"The hill is very important," said Sostschenko. "The general said so and the general's always right. There are too many men and too few hills." "I'll make you a present of the high ground," said a shadow. "Thank you."

He took the hill in both hands and carried it to the general. "A hero, a hero!" cried the general. He was in a steel pillbox and his voice came from inside. It echoed dully but it could be heard everywhere. Soldiers were building a wall around the pillbox. He groped his way carefully through them. He must be careful of the hill he was carrying. The soldiers were bleeding from many wounds. "Put the hill down and stand with your back to the entrance so that your body will protect me from the bullets when I accept the hill," ordered the general. He obeyed. The general quickly opened the door, seized the hill and slipped back once more into his pillbox. "You are a hero and I need heroes among my soldiers," said the general. He was attentive. The enemy attacked. "Do your duty and die," came the voice from the pillbox. The soldiers did their duty and died and the wall collapsed. "I'm coming to your aid," said the general, but the pillbox door did not open. "Have we the right to live?" asked the soldiers. "No," replied the general. "You must not break your oath." The enemy arrived in great numbers. "No one must surrender," came an angry voice from the pillbox. He received a blow and saw blood running from the wound. "Let me in," he implored. "Get back!" shouted the general. He was afraid of the general. He went on fighting, but his strength was ebbing. The enemy broke through the wall which was made of human bodies. Soldiers went on falling and the enemy drew ever closer to the pillbox. It was swimming in blood and the blood was mingled with a stream of tears. A host of children wept for the soldiers. The general in his pillbox covered his ears and asked: "Are they all dead?" "I am still alive," he had to admit. "Go on fighting until you die," ordered the general. Sostschenko crawled through the dead soldiers and did not reply when the general asked the question a second time. The enemy banged on the door of the pillbox. "I surrender," called the general, amiably. He saw him come out. The general was sweating for it was very hot in the pillbox. He left the hill lying where it was. He had forgotten it. . . .

Sostschenko could not breathe. He opened his eyes. Two candles were now burning in the foxhole. They had pulled one of the shadows into the light and had begun to undress him. His face was in the dark, and he whimpered with pain. They cut off his shirt. It was stiff with dirt. The hairy chest lay in the light of the candle. There was a sharp shrapnel splinter in his shoulder. They tore it out. The shadow howled. A stream of blood flowed from the open wound. A sinister silence. Sostschenko could hear the candle flame spluttering. . . .

He had bolted the door from the inside. The barracks were asleep except for the guard patrolling the corridor. A small light was burning over the icon. A spider crawled over the dormitory wall. The hundred lamps from the cathedral were reflected in the window panes; they were showing a new film in the nave. The spider came to rest on the icon. It seemed bewildered by this miracle of glass and gold; the red, green and mauve beads and the mysterious cross that resembled the emblem on its back. It drew up its spindly legs and remained there motionless. He knelt down as he had learned to do as a child. "Lord, give me a sign," he prayed, "a tiny sign that You are the truth. You are shrouded in mystery and eternity. Let something happen. Forgive my doubts." He folded his hands and looked down at them; they seemed unfamiliar and alien. No sign appeared. The icon did not move. The candles slowly guttered. The guard came up the corridor step by step, Sostschenko cast a glance at the bolt and saw that it was still in place. There was nothing to fear.

His heart stood still when there was a knock on the door. He made no answer and knelt there as though frozen. "Why don't you answer?" From outside came the voice of the commissar, not the guard. "I saw some light. What are you doing with the candles? Has the light bulb gone?" The commissar rattled at the bolt. "Now let the miracle hap-

pen," he prayed. His gaze wandered around the room looking for someplace to hide the icon. It was hopeless; the
cupboard had no door; the pallet was too high above the
ground. Four bare walls. No hiding place for God. The
rancid smell of candles in the air. The electric bulb in its
rusty socket hung pitilessly from the ceiling. The commissar knocked louder. Now he had to open up. His limbs
creaked as he stood up. As he drew the bolt the door was
pushed roughly back. "Oh!" cried the commissar in surprise. "An icon!" The candlelight flickered on his leather
coat. He waited for the collision between two worlds.
"An icon," repeated the commissar almost incredulously,
pulling the door gently behind him. It was as though they
were sharing a secret. The commissar pushed his fur cap
back from his forehead. "Can I look at it?" He was completely bewildered for he had expected abuse and mockery. "We used to have one," said the commissar reverently
running his finger over the picture. "I—it is only because
it's a work of art," he stammered. "It is more than that."

The commissar's fur cap cast a huge shadow on the wall.
The spider drew itself together for an attack, rolled up its
legs and flopped like a pebble to the floor. The commissar
went on stroking the icon. He crushed the insect with the
toe of his boot. "Where do your people live, comrade?"
"They're dead." "This is a memento, eh?" asked the commissar pointing to the icon. "I've had it for twelve years,"
he admitted. "Twelve years ago I was living in China"—
the commissar rummaged back in his past. "They worship
idols there." He blew his cheeks out as if he wanted to

show what an idol looked like. Sostschenko could not help smiling. "Don't laugh. Do you know what He looks like?" "Who?" "God." "I—I don't believe in Him." "But you're afraid of Him." "No, certainly not," he said trying to deny it.

"That accursed fear," said the commissar hanging the image back onto the wall, turning on the light and blowing out the candles. Now they stood in the stark electric light. The atmosphere of confidence and warmth was dispelled. "Sometimes it takes hold of us and we can't tell why," said the commissar emphatically. He ran his hand over his forehead as if he had come out of a hot room. "You can leave it hanging there. There are no orders forbidding this." Sostschenko defended himself desperately. "It doesn't mean anything to me. I already told you that I only keep it because of its value as I might keep a gold ring." He stopped and when he looked at the icon in the light of the electric bulb he recognized how tawdry the image was. The worthless glass beads, the gaudy face. His attitude towards the icon began to change. As it hung there on the bare wall it was merely a remnant of superstition. He felt insulted. "What are you thinking about?" asked the commissar. Sostschenko went over to the wall, took down the icon and turned it over and over irresolutely in his hands. The commissar paced thoughtfully up and down the room. He felt himself threatened by his cunning smile. "Nothing more than a means of suggestion," he said. "That's exactly what it is," replied the commissar. Sostschenko went over to the window and opened it just as the lights in the cathedral

went out. "I refuse to be influenced any more," he said, taking the icon and throwing it outside. Like a bird struck by an arrow the image landed with a thud on the paving stones and broke in pieces. He went back into the room and looked at the commissar. "Are you satisfied?" "Yes, I'm satisfied," replied the commissar—"but what about God?" In his leather jacket the man looked like a bronze statue. "His icons hang up there," he said pointing out of the window to the starry sky. "You're more dangerous than I thought," said the commissar furiously, banging the door behind him. Plaster trickled from the walls to the floor. . . .

A hand ran over his face. A mortar exploding outside had blown out the candles. A shadow wandered between the wounded men. Another shadow began to sing in the dark.

"Silence!" ordered Sostschenko. He undid his trousers and relieved nature. He felt the warm liquid running down his legs. What a satisfaction to be free of the pressure. The urine gradually grew cold. Sostschenko lay in his own filth. A layer of vapor hung over his loins. The acrid smell made his face tingle. . . .

Just as unappetizing had beeen the kitten crawling about in the mother cat's afterbirth. He had flung it through the air against the wall (or was it the icon?). The little skull burst like an eggshell and blood spurted over his hand. The mother cat began to wail pitifully and to slink after him along the street to the barracks. He looked for a stone but he could find nothing but a stick. He threatened her. She crouched in the street with fur raised. She spat at him as at a dog. He turned around and went on his way. The cat followed him at a safe distance. With a furtive glance at her over his shoulder, he whipped around suddenly and rushed at her. She crawled backwards on all fours. Green eyes staring at the stick. He had never seen a cat crawl backwards before. The distance became less. Now! The stick flew through the air, whizzed over her head and hit her tail. A shrill scream but the beast did not move from its position. Its arched back looked like a Cossack's sword. The slime she had licked from the kitten still stuck to her whiskers. She was incredibly repulsive. He could not bring himself to strangle her but it took courage to turn his back on her. Perhaps she would leap at him and dig her claws in his neck. He quickened his pace, and finally broke into a run. In dismay he looked around once or twice and each time the cat leaped after him. Out of breath he reached the barracks and banged the door. He felt better after a glass of vodka. From the darkness of the house he looked out into the street. The cat was crouching in the dusk, its eyes fixed on the door. He seized his gun. For some odd reason he could not get the beast in the sights. Moreover, the window pane hampered him and he dared not open the window for fear of the cat. He must take the risk of the glass. Placing a stool on the table, he laid the barrel across it. Now the cat's forehead came in his sights (or was it the icon?). The beast squatted motionless in the dusk and screamed. He could see its bared teeth. He put his finger on the trigger and pulled. The window pane broke; the cat somersaulted in the air and then lay lifeless. Sud-

denly he felt relieved. Then he noticed that the cat had clambered to its feet. It staggered and glared at the broken window. Its screams were loud and gruesome like those of a terrified child. It ran around in circles. He had to aim as it ran. Shot after shot raised the dust but he did not hit her (he did not hit the icon). A dog leaped out of the neighboring house with its tongue hanging out. He stopped shooting but the dog remained some distance away from the cat. It was afraid, and wriggled to and fro on its hindquarters as though it were suffering from worms. His hands were wet with sweat. He grabbed the vodka glass. The alcohol coursed through his head and suddenly everything was marvellous—the cat in its agony, the dog in its panic. He grabbed for his bayonet and hurried out. He hacked away at the cat until it lay lifeless. He wanted to kill the dog, too, but it had slunk away howling dismally. With satisfaction he looked at his handiwork. His uniform was covered with the cat's blood. Some Red soldiers had come up and were now looking at him and his victim. Despite his drunkenness he could clearly sense their disgust. He laughed, laughed loudly at the top of his lungs. . . .

The soldiers in the foxhole were looking for something. They shone a light on Sostschenko's face; they did it as though he were already a dead man. In the meanwhile he had become used to the stench of his urine. His trousers stuck to his thighs. It was more comfortable when he pressed his legs together closely. He dosed. The voices of the soldiers tore him out of his half-sleep. He could not understand what they said, but he realized that they were talking about him. The disgust with which they handled him betrayed their intention. As they dragged him through the corridor, a stab of pain ran through his hip. He tried in despair to dig his nails into the damp earth but they dragged him forward. For them he was already a corpse which had started to decay. The daylight fell on his ashen face. Accursed be the sun in which he would have to breathe his last gasp. He wanted to get back to the cave, where he was sheltered. Not to end like the cat in the dust. Not like the icon in the barracks courtyard. He felt remorse and disgust with himself. Had the icon given some sign at that time his life would have been quite different. The kitten would have lived. Accursed be that idol which had given no sign. . . .

Chapter Thirteen

From the west came a noise which could only be a plane. Then the silver bird appeared over the hill and made two or three circles above the devastated key position.

Against the sun Lieutenant Trupikow could barely distinguish the black crosses on the wings. White flares rose from the hopeless German position. He hoped that the reconnaissance plane would not see them in the harsh sunlight. He pressed closely to the wall of the trench and followed attentively each maneuver of the plane. It seemed to be less interested in the bare hill than in the silent front beyond the strip of marshy ground. In that direction there was suddenly an ominous silence. The tanks seemed to huddle on the ground like timorous beasts. The only sign of life was from the Germans where the hedgehog formed an obstacle between himself and the marsh line. They waved canvas sheets which fluttered wildly over their foxholes. They screamed and fired as though their din could be heard by the men in the plane.

The plane circled tirelessly, diving and then zooming again with a roar into the sky. When it flew over the skeleton of the pylon and the debris of the tank on the hill Lieutenant Trupikow hoped that it would turn away. But no, the machine was merely sniffing out the terrain. It returned. The lieutenant had an uncomfortable feeling. Finally he understood why the plane did not fly off. From the direction of Emga came a light throb which grew louder by the moment. Then he recognized the little dark patches in the sky. The air grew more oppressive. His own men behind the strip of marsh began to grow excited. The tanks started to crawl helplessly. Red soldiers scuttled in all directions like insects. Trupikow heard the defense guns go into action with dull explosions which left little puffs of cloud in the sky. The squadron had broken formation and the machines were now playing follow the leader.

The reconnaissance plane sheered off as though it had nothing to do with the affair, until a salvo of rockets hissed from its silver belly. The rockets sped fanwise onto the sector behind the strip of marsh. Lieutenant Trupikow was ashamed of the sense of relief he felt. Now he knew the objective of the attack; no rockets came in the direction of his position. With the certainty of a hawk the first machine from the squadron now dived past the little puffs of black onto the marsh. Directly above his trench it would pull out of the dive. A gruesome siren-like wail rang out. Trupikow was defenseless, delivered over to this diving plane. Frozen with terror he saw the fuselage with the swept-back wings hurtling down on him. He saw the bombs leave the belly of the Stuka and speed forward in the direction of its flight. Now it was the bombs which terrified him. It was almost incredible that the bombs swept over his trench and did not fall on the Germans either but landed exactly where the rockets had fallen—in the marsh sector. Dirt swirled through the air, a rain of muck and smoke. The billowing of the explosions reached the lieutenant together with the clatter of the plane's machine guns. An invisible fist seemed to press him against the earth. Then another wailing. Once more a greedy snout sped down towards him. The screaming sirens tore at his nerves. One machine after another dove down, dropped its bomb. The earth behind the marsh seemed to burst. A gun carriage sailed through the air like a flying carpet. As though carried by the wind a tank turret sailed over the bushes. It came almost circumspectly to earth again.

The lieutenant saw no men in this hell. They seemed to have been swallowed by the fountains of dirt. But the tanks and all those who were still alive behind the stretch of marsh refused to die without a struggle. From various positions the light antiaircraft guns began to bark. A hail of bullets rose to meet the whining airplanes. The machine guns in the tanks answered the machine guns in the planes. A ghastly spectacle which the Germans also watched, spellbound, from their trench. Lieutenant Trupikow sobbed with rage while before his eyes one of his own tank detachments, and with it all hope of rescue, was blown into the air. He pressed his face into the earth until an enormous explosion made him look up. A huge scarlet flame and a mushroom of smoke rose skywards. Wet lumps of earth rattled down into the trench. The antiaircraft guns had hit one of the Stukas, the last man in the formation. The crackling fell silent. The heavy antiaircraft sent a few forlorn shots after the departing Stukas. Then they too ceased firing. The silence weighed on Trupikow. On the sloping ground ahead of him lay the jagged trench occupied by the Germans. In no man's land he could see an aluminum wing as high as a house; in the distance it looked like a statue. Behind him and behind the marsh a volcanic landscape. Steam swept across the ground, black oily smoke wreathed itself round the crippled steel wrecks. Here and there a gun barrel, naked and helpless, pointed to the sky. A bush burned like a heap of straw and figures dashed about aimlessly between the craters. No, there was nothing more to expect from that direction. The lieutenant looked back towards the west. There lay the hill—the desolate hill with the steel skeleton and the two destroyed tanks. No trace of the victorious shock troops. The objective had not been reached. Plans, timetables, objectives and orders had all fallen through. Death reigned supreme on Hill 308. The Germans and he, Lieutenant Trupikow with his men, two doomed detachments facing death. As among merchants, one should have been able to barter.

The lieutenant slipped down into the trench. He paid no attention to the dead man whose outstretched hand banged against his boot. One question tortured him. How could he get back with his men? Across the open country? The German machine guns would mow them down. The only way was through the German hedgehog. He was com-

174

pelled to give the order for hand to hand fighting, to avenge his wounded men.

The first bullets whistled over the earth parapet which afforded him cover. In the distance too the firing flared up again. He walked to the entrance of the dugout not quite sure what course to take. A Red soldier was being carried past—one of the youngsters who had been sent straight from school to the battalion. One of his feet dragged along the trench wall. On the boy's face he could read the surprise of those who suffer a painless death. Trupikow watched how each of the two stretcher bearers grabbed one arm and one foot of the corpse. They swung the body to and fro, up into the air and over the parapet. Now he lay out there with his face turned towards the Germans. A bullet spat viciously in the earth near the dead boy. The next one hit the steel helmet, which clattered back into the trench. When a third bullet found the target the lieutenant wondered what good the Germans thought they were doing. He found it gruesome. The dead boy's face was no longer a face. The bullets ploughed into the body as into a target on a shooting range. Five, six, seven, he counted, in bewilderment. He grabbed for a gun. There were plenty of them lying around. Cautiously he pushed the barrel over the parapet. The puff of smoke from the enemy's rifle showed where he was. The glittering metal in the livid midday sun must be his weapon. Behind it a brighter patch: a face. He aimed carefully but the bullet landed in something green. It's pointless, he thought. It's pointless dealing with them. They're like wild beasts. One must kill them or be killed. There was no other choice.

The major leaned against the wall of the trench in the same state as he had come out of the marsh—barefoot, with torn off shoulder straps and a big slit in his tunic. His hands and face were encrusted with blood and dirt; he could shake the encrusted mud off himself like a fragile shell. He grasped the butt of the rifle ready to shoot whenever his inflamed eyes found a target, ready to fight, to beat and to strangle. Only one thing bothered him: the mosquitoes. Hosts of mosquitoes swarmed in the trench. A shimmering blue mist of little bodies and tiny stings. Greedy for blood. A plague against which he was utterly defenseless. They crawled over his neck, flew into his face, slipped under his armpits, settled on his naked feet. Little bright primordial monsters. They landed on his skin. Their proboscises turned dark with blood. They sucked till the flat of his hand came down on them and shattered their little blood-filled bodies. They sacrificed their lives for the enjoyment of a few seconds, but they left behind an itch, a stinging pain, small bumps. The bites lay like a scarf around his collar, around his wrists and ankles. It was worse than a salvo of mortars, which at least for a time would have driven them away. He licked the bites on his hands but he could do nothing about his feet and neck.

He had wanted to be in this mess and now here he was involved in everything a sick brain could conceive. But worse than all the stench of corruption, the hopelessness, the filth, the itching and the mosquitoes, were his own men. They had received him like lost travellers who had just come across the first sign of human life, but gradually his presence had poisoned the air. What the tank shells, the hissing salvoes, had not been able to accomplish he had accomplished: to break their morale.

The men accepted his command with stony faces. They observed him suspiciously as though he were preparing for their funeral. It was of no avail that he handed over the command to the sergeant. The hatred was still there. Now he was afraid of them. At least they made him feel uncomfortable. He, for whom life no longer had any meaning, who had wanted to sacrifice it for them, now began to love it.

Here between the rage of the enemy and the hatred of his own men his life appeared of value once more. The grief over his dead child and the memory of his wife faded into the background. In this crater landscape he suddenly discovered that there was nothing more important than himself. In front of him the bombed terrain, the wing of the Stuka sticking out of the ground like a splinter; behind him the labyrinth of saps with the cut-off group of Russians. Further to the rear the hill, lifeless, cold and alien like another planet. But he was still alive—a filthy creature with naked feet, tattered uniform, mutilated hands, sagging cheeks and an ashen skin. His grey face and feverish eyes were reflected in all the other faces and eyes in this trench. Lonely, desperate men, already envying each other the tobacco dust in their pockets, a slice of bread as hard as a stone, a handful of bullets salvaged from the mud. During the Stuka attack on the strip of marsh they had been a unit once more. They had given blood-curdling yells and waved the rags they wore on their own bodies. And then came the disappointment when the squadron disappeared over the horizon, as though they had been waiting for something more, a mere sign: WE'VE SEEN YOU! STICK IT OUT! WE'RE COMING.

But no sign came. They remained behind, abandoned to the immensity of the battlefield, expecting at any moment that from in front or behind them a brown wave of human bodies would rush yelling madly in a pandemonium of whining shrapnel, the car-r-rump of tank shells and the twitter of steel-jacketed bullets. But no, nothing happened. An oppressive silence. In addition, weariness, hunger and the mosquitoes. No bandages, no water and, worst of all, no ammunition. The dwindling supplies had escaped their notice in the excitement. The ammunition bearer who hurried between the two machine guns was the first to realize it.

Ammo! The cry echoed through the winding trench to the foxhole. From the foxhole a man roared: "Surrender! Put out white rags!" and the man blazed away like a lunatic. Shot after shot. Careful aim. Shouts at each hit. The sergeant cursed him into silence. His steel helmet rolled along the trench and reached the major.

"We must take a vote," said the sergeant. He was panting. The major saw in the sergeant too a reflection of his own ashen face. "We must let them choose, sir. No one will obey orders any more. To be taken prisoner or a break through. The last possibility." The major bit the ball of his hand. The skin was peeling and the mosquito poison burned like fire.

He evaded the issue. "You're in command," he said.

"All right!" replied the sergeant. "Break-through, or taken prisoner?" He held his revolver with the muzzle pointed at the major as though he wanted to force out the answer.

The major bit his finger and asked: "Do you think we could get away with a break-through?" Blood oozed from the bites down to his finger tips. He bit more viciously.

"Yes," said the sergeant. "God be damned if it doesn't succeed!"

The major shook the blood from his hand. "Majority decision, eh?"

"Yes, Herr Major."

"That was not an order."

"I take it to be." The sergeant plunged his revolver muzzle into the trench wall. The barrel was full of earth. A shot would blow his hand to pieces. "Your answer!" he suddenly shouted at the major. "Prisoner or break-through?"

"I don't count." The major saw the wounded Russian officer lying in a break in the parapet near the dugout. They had just thrown him out. He could not distinguish his face but he saw that one of the wounded man's hands was digging into the earth.

"You must decide," insisted the sergeant. "You must be the first. I've no time to lose. We're wasting our last ammunition."

The major remained silent.

"I need your vote!" the sergeant persisted.

No time, no ammunition. Break out or suicide. Taken prisoner or suicide. These were the alternatives. The major bit his hand again. A fragmentation shell burst overhead. "I must stand aside from any decision," said the major. The wounded Russian had tumbled from his resting place. He could no longer see his hand. There would be no prisoner of war camp for him.

"Herr Major!" threatened the sergeant. "To break out or be taken prisoner?"

"Won't you get it through your head that I can't take part in this vote?"

The sergeant looked at his mud-stained revolver barrel. He banged it empty on his elbow. The earth trickled over the major's bare feet. It was like the touch of a hand. "I insist on an answer!"

"Very well then—taken prisoner." The major's teeth bit once more into his hand. The pain of the bite ran through his whole body. He could no longer feel the burning mosquito bites. His bare feet were icy cold. The sergeant looked at him. It was his own face staring at him but now it was filled with hatred. He felt the sergeant's gaze as he stood there without insignia, barefoot, with torn tunic, filthy hands and bloody rings of bumps around his throat and wrists.

"Coward!" shouted the sergeant turning away.

The major was not offended by the insult. Had he not just now decided to take his own life, he would have been proud of it. He began to consider how he should do it. He had no revolver. Should he take a piece of wire and put the barrel of a rifle into his mouth? The Russians in the sap ceased firing. It was almost peaceful. The sergeant was already talking to the first sentry.

"Break-through or surrender?"

"What does the major choose?" asked the sentry.

"Break-through."

"Good. Then we break through," replied the man.

"It's a lie!" the major wanted to shout, but he could not get the words out. The sergeant's steel helmet wandered on. The major was looking for a piece of wire or a cord, but all he could find was a leather strap. As he loaded the gun he suddenly noticed how quiet the Russians were at the former company headquarters. Perhaps they too had used up all their ammunition. Perhaps he should have voted for a break-through after all. The idea that he might kill himself shortly before a decisive turn of events disturbed him. As he fastened the strap to the trigger guard his hand was trembling. He forced all other thoughts out of his mind. The important thing was to be dead immediately. The bullet must go through the upper jaw into his brain. He would feel no pain. He put the gun between his legs to see whether he could fire it with his toes. As he caught sight of his feet he realized how revolting he would look as a dead man—a shattered skull and a filthy body.

It would be a good thing that no one would see him. As an officer, moreover, he was entitled to a coffin. If he were lucky they would bury him in a hole. It was a consoling thought that he was leaving no one behind, neither wife nor child. He wanted to fall with his face toward the ground; he must lean forward a little. The barrel under his chin stared at him like a dead eye. Suddenly voices came from the foxhole. He heard his name mentioned. "If he hadn't come they would still be alive." He still wanted to learn the reason for their hatred. "When the captain called on us to surrender there were more of us. He has five men on his conscience." Then once more the voice of the sergeant. Obviously there was a fight going on. The voices grew louder. "Equal rights for all. You can't overrule me." The sergeant replied something incomprehensible. "Well shoot then, go ahead and shoot!" screamed the voice. "You think I wouldn't waste a bullet on you?" said the sergeant. And the other: "Surrender, whether the major likes it or not."

A shot rang out through the trench. Five and one makes six, thought the major. The muzzle between his legs still stared at him. He should have remained in Podrowa. He remembered his telephone conversation with Division. His order: Counter attack on the hill. Had that been only yesterday? The thirty replacements he had sent up to this position and the dead driver in the Podrowa cemetery. . . . A single day's results which could be laid at his door. And how many similar days lay behind him? He bent over the gun with his mouth wide open. The cold steel touched his gums. Clumsily he felt with his foot for the strap. Would he feel anything in the end?

"Herr Major!"

He jerked up and leaned the rifle with embarrassment against the trench wall. The sergeant stood before him.

"They have voted unanimously to break out."

The major stared at his naked feet. The sergeant caught sight of the gun and the strap attached to the trigger guard.

Lieutenant Trupikow entered the dugout. The German captain sat with his head in his hands at the table made of ammunition boxes.

"Haven't they surrendered yet, *Herr Leutnant?*" he said, trying to look anxious. He made no mention of the Stuka attack.

"No, they haven't." What a beast, thought the lieutenant. In a cage he behaves like a human being but when he's got a gun in his hand he shoots at corpses. What does this wolf with a sheep's face want here? His own country has enough hills like these. I've seen them, green trees, rivers and clean little villages. On their roads you find neither mud nor trash and the corn stands like soldiers in their fields. Yet they envy us a few marshy forests, the parched steppes and a few wooden huts. The lieutenant worked himself into a rage. He would shoot the German. That was the obvious solution. A shot in the back of the neck so that he would not have to look him in the face. When the head is bent slightly forward it is impossible to miss the spine and there is no chance of hearing the victim's cry. Even before death takes place the nerves to the vocal cords have beeen broken. An ideal method of execution. He observed his victim. He has a very short neck, he thought professionally. Strange from what aspects one could examine a neck. The German's high collar, however, irritated him. Perhaps he could persuade him to take off his jacket. No, he must shoot him outside; he would have to take the jacket into account. But suppose the revolver misfired? He could of course order the sergeant to do it. Trupikow looked at the sergeant fixedly; if only he could read his thoughts. And then suddenly he gave the order: "In half an hour we're going to attack the German position. The signal will be a red flare. All squads will take their wounded with them. Pass the word down."

"Signal for attack, red flare. Wounded to be taken along," repeated the sergeant.

The lieutenant pointed to the German.

The hint was clear enough but the sergeant ran outside. The opportunity had been missed. "We must have another try," said the lieutenant, paying great attention to his German accent.

"What?" asked the captain.

"In half an hour it will all be over."

"What?" repeated the German.

Then we'll leap at each other's throats, thought the lieutenant, but he said: "Our tanks will smoke them out with flame throwers. Come, after all they're your men."

"I've thought it over," replied the German. "I can't do

it." He spoke carefully as a man speaks to a dog when he does not know whether it is vicious or harmless.

"Why not?" He only wanted to get the German outside the dugout with his back to him and his neck within range. This hesitation upset his plans.

"Why not? You did it before."

The German shook his head. "Do you know who's with them?"

"No."

"The C.O."

"So what?"

"The lone soldier who got through your lines is my commanding officer."

The lieutenant's interest was aroused by this enemy whom he would see in half an hour's time. So they do have men like that too, he thought: a commanding officer who joins his troops during a battle. "What difference does it make?" he asked impatiently. His time was running out. He must make up his mind.

"He warned me," said the captain, "that later he would call me to account."

So he's afraid, thought Trupikow with some relief. He's afraid of his C.O. He stared hard into the candle flame.

A pit in the woods. Dark bushes and stunted firs. An angry sun setting between the tree tops. Prisoners outside the pit, one next to the other, their eyes fixed on the prepared grave. Not a word from their lips. Not a word from the detachment of Red soldiers. "Kneel down!" orders the commissar in German. The prisoners don't want to under-

stand. The safety catch of a revolver clicks. A prisoner grinds his teeth; a crunch as though his jaw has broken. A dirt clod works loose from the wall and plops into the grave. The commissar then goes from one prisoner to the next. He does it efficiently as though he has never done anything else in his life. Each shot echoes in the tree tops. The prisoners fall forward one after the other. As the last one falls to the ground it is night. Only a glimmer above them betrays the sky.

No, the temptation was strong but horrible. And time was running out. Another few minutes and then at least the anxiety of waiting would be over.

Some Red soldiers carried stretchers into the dugout. From the beds came the quiet moaning of the wounded. Weapons were loaded and the Siberians hung bags full of hand grenades around their necks. The dugout with its smell of carbolic, damp, and candle grease seemed to be quite cozy. There was a feeling of farewell in the air—farewell to security, farewell to life. With each stretcher they carried out, the oppression and fear grew. One man after another entered the bay, hesitant, buoying himself up with the desperate hope that the enemy bullet might hit the man next to him.

"I'll be brief," said Lieutenant Trupikow. "Our position . . ." he did not quite know how to express himself. "For some time we have been cut off. . . . We must fight our way out and you must come with us."

The captain looked at him blankly. Suddenly he had a

glimmer of understanding. "That's impossible. But you said . . . your word of honor." He was speechless and suddenly felt that he had been cheated of his approaching deliverance. A prison camp surrounded by barbed wire . . . no shells . . . no fear of death . . . peace. Everything was swept away. "Leave me here," he begged—"It's pointless. Try to understand my position." His incoherent babble met with a stony face. "I could look after your wounded. . . . Really I could." He spoke like a child who has not yet learned to lie.

In the meanwhile the dugout had emptied. As though they were now superfluous the candles began to gutter in their little holders. Wick after wick hissed and went out. Only one now remained alight, a signpost to death. A human bundle was left on the bed. His breathing ticked like a clock but he did not move. He had been forgotten, like the rickety table, the empty food tins, a crust of bread, the remains of jam, scraps of paper and broken weapons.

"Come!" ordered the lieutenant.

The captain stood up behind the table. "What about him?" he asked pointing to the bundle.

The lieutenant did not reply. They went out into the trench, the Russian keeping close on the heels of his prisoner. They pushed aside the canvas flap across the entrance and stood in the trench. The bright sunlight blinded them like a flash of lightning.

"*Stoi!*" ordered the lieutenant. The captain stood still. It was as though he had felt a revolver muzzle in his back.

He turned around in terror and saw a bottle-shaped bomb in the lieutenant's hand. The Russian was fiddling with the cord.

"No!" screamed the German in terror.

The lieutenant looked up in surprise still holding the live hand grenade. "You mustn't do it," rang in his ears. He looked bewildered at his hand and threw the grenade over the parapet where it exploded. He had intended to throw it into the dugout. All right he would not be a beast. "You stay here!" said the lieutenant, pointing to the dug-out. "Get going. Inside, inside! *Dawei! Dawei!*" he screamed and rushed off almost with relief along the trench. The distance between them increased. Two points in an endless grey expanse. The Russian marched in the regulation step of a platoon on its way to an execution.

A red flare rose in the sky from above the Russian occu-pied trenches. Green steel helmets and brown figures poured out of them. The sergeant put his whistle to his lips. Hubbub on both sides. The whine of bullets.

"Let them come nearer," shouted the sergeant. The fir-ing ceased. A single Russian tommy gun hammered away across no man's land. Then it too fell silent. The major laid his rifle on the parapet and the sergeant put the last clip in his revolver. They leaned side by side against the dirt wall.

An officer ran at the head of the Russians with arms

raised as though he were showing his troops the way. Behind him stumbled the stretcher bearers carrying the wounded. They drew nearer and still no shots came from the trench. Disturbed by the unusual silence the men lagged behind the officer. Suddenly they wheeled to the right. The officer ran forward while his men made off towards the unoccupied trenches.

"They're not obeying him," shouted the sergeant. The enemy wave became a drawn-out column trying to find a way over the open ground, making for cover with rifles lowered and faces towards the trench. The crew of a heavy machine gun was dragging a tripod. The stretcher bearers followed behind, stumbling and staggering to their feet again. Their loads swayed. Only the officer surged forward. He didn't look back.

"Don't shoot!" ordered the major. "Don't shoot!" His words were passed along the trench. They saw the file of men scurrying across the open country and the running officer. The one figure grew ever clearer while the others became little brown shadows in the distance. Now they could make out the steel helmet, then the grey holster and finally his distorted face. He ran towards the foxhole. At the spot where he would reach the trench squatted two sappers. He loomed up over the parapet large as a giant, broad shoulders, a stranger from another world. He sprang with raised arms into the trench. The dull thud of a rifle butt. A death rattle. Then silence. In the distance they could see for some time yet a ghostly file of men which

189

finally disappeared into the shell-pitted lower slopes. The major and the sergeant looked at each other.

"Can you understand that?"

"A miracle," replied the major. They still could not grasp what had actually happened.

"Now we can go back," said the sergeant at last. "We can go back." He seized the major's hand and shook it. With broad grins they slapped each other on the back. Their grey faces and glazed eyes began to light up. They staggered as if they were drunk. The gun with the strap attached to the trigger slipped down from the breastwork. Behind them in the trench, too, voices were raised. A tear ran down the major's cheek like a trickle through a crust of dirt. Mud-stained figures hurried up and surrounded the major. Cigarettes were passed around. Corpses were still lying there and the smell of the dead still clung to their uniforms. But they seemed to have forgotten that the tanks still stood behind the barbed wire, that they were still a long way from their own front line. The labyrinth of saps, the foot-path through the undergrowth, the devastated high ground. On the lower ground the marshy forest. And somewhere, in impenetratable undergrowth, the enemy. . . .

The major thought about the retreat as he walked along the trench. Only now was he able to look around and realize where he was. In the stranglehold grip of fear, the trench had been only a barren cleft in the earth—a small ravine full of filth, blood and human bodies. When the saps to the rear of them were empty, clarity again returned. Details leaped to notice, instead of vague outlines.

A pile of empty cartridge cases. The little balls from the trigger cords of the hand grenades, white as moth balls. The broken tripod of a machine gun. A steel helmet with a gaping hole. A naked human foot without a leg, waxen as a model in a chiropodist's window. A little further off, a head hung over the parapet. Arched eyebrows like a carnival mask of a Mongolian. The compressed-air tank of a flame thrower. In one of the bays a rigid arm which they had to push aside but which moved back behind them like the arm of a turnstile. The soggy ground. Noiseless footsteps treading on corpses covered by only a thin layer of earth. A coil of broken telephone wire. A dead man leaning against the wall as though crucified. But the major did not notice the mosquitoes any more. The bluish swarms hung like a veil in the air, pursued him along the trench as though he were a piece of carrion to be devoured. And then the wounded. They came crawling out of the foxhole. Faltering speech. Dripping bandages. Glazed eyes. Imploring gestures. He had to reassure them that they would not be left behind; had to promise them that stretchers would be made. He looked at the badly wounded Russian captain and knew that he dared not tell him the truth: that even the unwounded would be lucky to reach their own lines. That the bearers in case of danger would drop their loads in the marsh. He raised hopes that he could not fulfill. He lied, perhaps from compassion, perhaps from cowardice.

He gave his orders for the retreat calmly and circumspectly. The order of march. Distributing the rest of the ammunition. There was no sense in leaving these commands to the sergeant now. As they marched off the sun stood like a red disc behind the skeleton of the pylon. The major led the way. He pushed aside the dead men barring the entrance to the sap and saw on either side only the dirt walls of the trench. They skirted a destroyed machine-gun nest. On catching sight of the dead Russian he thought it must be the spot from which the captain had spoken. The major did not expect to see him still alive.

When he recognized him, leaning pale and motionless against the wrecked tank, he thought he was dead and so he passed him in silence. So many dead men whom he knew had stared at him in the same way. The captain leaned there in the shadow and the major was dazzled by the sun. A corpse is not a pleasant sight. The major did not think of either punishment or blame, nor of what he would have done if the captain had still been alive. He felt only compassion. He thought of the high ground which lay ahead, of the path through the marsh and the oppressive feeling of responsibility. His bare feet trembled from weakness. He was tortured by thirst and felt a sharp pain in his lungs.

The sergeant who was following close on the major's heels stared at the captain as though he had seen a ghost. He had been paying attention to the major, and then an almost unnoticeable movement on the part of the captain caught his eye. He recognized him. He was so terrified and bewildered that in his excitement he could not utter a word and automatically did exactly what the major had done. He passed by without a word.

The captain let the rest of his company go past. It was a long grey line, longer than he had dared hope. Familiar faces bearing the marks of privation. He smiled at them. He could have embraced each of these mud-stained figures. His joy at seeing them again was genuine. He was happy. He stood up, pushed his steel helmet to the back of his head. His eyes gleamed until the last man had gone past. No one had looked at him. No word of recognition, not even a nod. Not a sign, either, from the bearers who passed him carrying the wounded. He felt that he had been buried alive.

He had to sit down on the broken tank track. His hands trembled and his feet were numb. He stared vacantly at the high ground. In the evening sun everything had taken on a bluish red tinge—the steel plates to which he held for support, the trench with its earthen walls, the undergrowth below the hill, the men whose figures were now growing smaller in the distance, the shell-pitted landscape of the lower slope. He pulled himself together with difficulty and lowered his feet carefully to the ground. He felt his way slowly forward, step by step. His hands held on to the sap walls for support. He stumbled unheedingly past his dug-out. He had forgotten that a wounded man was still lying inside. He was a pariah. Even the dead over whom he scrambled no longer meant anything to him. He did not realize that he was leaving his position for the last time. He stumbled on in silence until the sound of a man panting caught his ear. This panting drew his attention to a face, and the face to a bloodstained uniform of a Russian captain. Only with difficulty did these details form into a picture.

"*Woda!*" implored Sostschenko. He had sensed that someone was near at hand. In distress the captain stared at him. He had understood the word water but he was not even carrying a field canteen.

"*Woda!*" implored the Russian with a faint movement of the hand. The captain took hold of this hand although he had to overcome his distaste. Two pariahs, two dying men consoling each other. Absent-mindedly he stroked the blood-stained hand.

"Sonja!" whispered Sostchenko.

The captain thought he understood this but the words that followed from the foam-flecked lips escaped him. *If you chance upon the icon, give it poison. Always carry the poison with you. You can never be sure when the cat will come.* The captain reproached himself for not being able to understand a word. A cigarette, he thought. They had not even left him a cigarette! No, this man was beyond help. The rattle in his throat died. He was not dead yet but he had begun to smell of decay. The flies settled blood-thirstily on his lips and the captain spread his handkerchief over Sostschenko's face.

He stumbled along and soon had already forgotten him. He also forgot about the saps which offered him cover and the footpath that would have led him to his goal. Branches lashed him in the face. Mosquitoes settled on his forehead. He ran aimlessly through the undergrowth. A tick-tock rang in his ears. He paid no attention. Ahead of him lay the rising moon-landscape of the high ground—a shimmering blue expanse with dark circular holes. Ahead on the hill figures were running. Some of them were carrying tripods. Possibly his men. He was indifferent. The tick-tock grew constantly wilder. The figures flew like dots to the horizon. Many of them disappeared with a leap into the void. The sky turned blood red and the earth became a deep blue. The captain left the cover of the undergrowth. He came to a spring with small pebbles rattling from it. He placed one foot before the other, swaying like a drunken man. What have I done, he wondered. His thoughts were confused, mere fragments of questions breaking through his befogged memory. One single concept kept recurring: justice. He could not have said what he actually meant by it.

A strip of wire lay in his path. He stumbled and fell. Now he lay on the ground and saw the hill from a different perspective. The light played on undulating valleys and the shell holes formed picturesque volcanoes. There were gentle slopes and little ravines. As far as his eyes reached he could find nothing to distress him. The trickle from a puddle seemed to him like a lake. He had solved the question of justice. There were different aspects of it, he decided. As he struggled to his feet he muttered his thoughts aloud. The words echoed like an axiom. He remembered vaguely that this wisdom was already age-old. In his sloth he had so far made no use of it. One must try to understand everything. This thought suddenly became crystal clear. He had missed a great deal in life.

He stood up and went on his way. Those of the bright living dots which had not disappeared from sight had reached the crest of the hill. He and the whistling shrapnel splinters were the only things moving on the terrain.

A turned-over stretcher lay in his path. It tempted him to sit down on it, to wait and see what would happen, to see if a shrapnel splinter would hit him. But suddenly he noticed congealed blood on the strap. He had had enough blood. It was better if the bullet hit him from behind. His back would make a good target.

He slowed down. It was worthwhile, being free of fear. Now he knew enough and there was no further need for him to run for his life. A few years or a single day bestowed on man—what was it really worth?

At last the bullet came. It did not hurt him. Just a light blow on his back. The hill, the broken pylon and the red sky sank into darkness. He fell into a shell hole with his face to the ground. The water entered his mouth. His last thought was: is this that justice?

Chapter Fourteen

W<small>HEN</small> the runner woke up it was night. The first-aid station seemed deserted. He could hear foreign voices and drunken laughter coming from one of the neighboring tents. He was frozen and his bare feet were stiff with cold. The overcoat which stank of disinfectant covered only the upper part of his body. In the distance flares were bursting in the sky. He felt abandoned and wanted to get up. When he heard the patter of footsteps he pulled the coat over his face. The steps drew closer and someone stood at his side. He held his breath and immediately the back of his skull started to hurt again. His chest was on fire and he was terrified. A hand fingered the coat and pulled it back.

"Sostschenko!" whispered a woman's voice. It sounded like a sob.

He held his breath again and made no reply. The sobbing wandered away. A mad woman, he thought. Flares played in the sky. Since no one bothered about him he stood up. Laboriously and in great pain. The foreign voices in the tent made him realize what he had to do. He had to go back. He must return to the place where they spoke his own language. He staggered rather than walked. At each step he felt needles tearing in his knees. His breath hammered, and he had to take his time. In the darkness lay the embankment along which he felt his way, the only landmark by which he could steer. It was like a black wall. His naked feet touched some metal. He recoiled and remembered that the guns must be here somewhere. With the danger of being discovered he forgot his pain. He wondered whether he ought to throw the coat away. If he fell into their hands again with this coat his number would be up, but he had lost his tunic and it was cold. Perhaps in his Russian coat the enemy would not recognize him immediately. He must think of everything.

The sky began to turn grey. Now he had to be doubly cautious. When he recognized the guns he breathed a sigh of relief. He was on the right path. He heard footsteps and once he saw a light. As he crawled along the ground he felt that he would never reach the end of this gun position. The row of guns stretched out without end. His apprehension made him careless. He stood up and ran. Although he could feel the salt taste of sweat on his lips, cold shudders ran down his spine. He had felt exactly the same when as a runner he had had to cross the marshy strip by night.

"*Stoi!*"

The sentry's shout hit him like a body blow. His feet stuck to the ground. With a jerk he pushed himself on. He cleared every obstacle that stood in his way—bushes, barbed wire and a pile of empty cartridge cases. He cursed the breaking dawn and waited for the bullet that seemed inevitable. When he noticed that his strength was ebbing he surrendered to his fate. Automatically he placed one foot before the other. He went quite slowly. But everything remained quiet behind. No one pursued him. At last he dared to rest. Panting heavily he squatted on the ground. His hands were trembling. Then came a new fright: no more flares. He was lost, irretrievably lost. Suddenly he giggled like a child; he had forgotten the embankment. Under cover of the slope he naturally could not see the flares. He crawled resolutely up the slope and grew calmer as soon as he saw the flares once more. It was like making land after a stormy trip at sea. Feeling more confident he slipped down the other side. The wounds in his legs had opened and the warm blood trickled down his legs. He did not bother to inspect them. He thought he could hear the murmur of a brook. He looked around suspiciously to both sides and continued to run. The sound of water grew stronger. There must be a river hereabouts and he wanted to be sure. It was not the sound of water but the muffled murmur of men. He listened carefully. He wanted to shout. German voices! Then his suspicion was aroused again. But no, it couldn't be a mistake. Another word he could understand! Doubled up, he crawled forward. A small bush interrupted his view so he pulled the branches aside: a slow moving mass. Tired, exhausted figures, talking his language. He felt sick. Prisoners. Living corpses that disappeared into the darkness.

He decided to stop playing the role of a hunted beast and to put some system into his flight. The first thing to do was to get hold of a weapon. He climbed up the slope again. Somewhere here must be the place from which they had flung him down, as well as the dugout in which they had interrogated him. If only he could surprise a sentry . . .

"*Kto a kto!*"

The runner remembered a call he had once heard. "*Si! ajo!*" he called back. He felt safe in his coat and in the half light.

"*Ajo!*" echoed the sentry's voice.

The man was standing directly above him on the slope. Instinctively he put out his hands, caught hold of two feet and pulled them sharply downwards. The body above him fell and he sprang to one side. He had no wish to roll down the slope together with the Russian. He was only interested in his weapon. He climbed up to where the sentry had stood and groped about the earth. There was no haste in his movements. He had plenty of time. He felt sure that he would find a gun here, and he found one. Now I have a gun, he thought, and the sentry is in my power. There's enough time to commit a murder. If I killed him now it would be a murder because I already have the gun. If I did not have it yet, it would be self-defense.

While he was trying out the weapon the sentry for some strange reason climbed up the slope again, without saying a word. Probably he had not understood what had happened. In the darkness the runner saw a shapeless shadow making towards him. He aimed. This would be his revenge. He shot and missed. The Russian began to scream. Let him scream. . . .

The runner turned and the low ground lay before him like a dark carpet. Lightning flashes gleamed overhead. Red and white lights flared up only to fade and change their positions. They reminded him of rail network at a train depot at night; he might have been standing at a level crossing looking at a maze of signal lights. The shouting sentry brought him back to reality. They won't get me, thought the runner.

He looked once more at the sector where the flares were rising and noticed that a part of it still remained dark. A gap in the signal system as though part of the apparatus was out of action. He set out in this exact direction. From the downward sloping country, into a maze of undergrowth. The ground under his feet gave and now he seemed to be running over a thick carpet. A sign that he was approaching the marsh. He thought he recognized the outlines of a dilapidated hut. Then another low building. Suddenly he knew what they were. Tanks. He had reached the forward position. Somewhere in the darkness a sentry must be standing. A fever of apprehension took hold of him. He made his way carefully towards one of the monsters. He would wait under cover of the steel walls until the sentry betrayed himself by some noise. Leaning against the cold metal he heard the deep breathing of a sleeping man; it came from inside the monster. A trap door must be open somewhere. How odd to be able to wait here in peace. His hand was touching the steel of a weapon, the appearance of which had always made him panic. He felt that he must do some harm to the sleeping monster. Like a child wishing to take its revenge he filled the exhaust pipes with dirt. He was too weary to do anything more, but his satisfaction was nevertheless enormous.

In the eerie light of a flare he saw Hill 308 for the first time from the enemy's viewpoint—a mighty mass of earth that towered menacingly above him. Now he understood why it had been so bitterly contested. It would not take him long now to reach the front line. Shell holes yawned in the earth ahead. In the air hung the nauseating stench of death. His feet sank into the slime. He remembered the coat and flung it into a puddle. A few more steps and he was standing in the barbed wire. Not a sound. His own position—the trench, the maze of saps, the machine-gun nests—lay abandoned. He pressed the gun to his chest and crawled nearer. The trench at last. With a feeling of exhilaration he jumped in. Nothing but dead men. He was too exhausted to find out whether the sergeant lay among them. He felt that he had suffered in vain—fear, flight, humiliation, wounds and this second flight. If the sergeant had got away with his life he could have saved himself all the trouble.

He stripped a corpse of its overcoat, tunic and boots. Dressed in the garments of a dead man he stumbled on in the direction where he thought the main fighting line was.

Chapter Fifteen

THE town commandant at Emga turned down the light of the paraffin lamp and directed the metal mirror toward the empty chair in front of his table. Then he turned to his orderly.

"Bring me the cavalry officer!"

He looked at the empty chair on which the light of the lamp fell. It could almost be an electric chair, he thought. In this case it would be better to have his victim sitting with his face to the wall so that he would not notice when he pulled the switch. His gaze fell on a list lying on the table and he noticed a spelling mistake. He felt ashamed because it was in his own handwriting and altered it quickly. Suppose someone had read it! He squashed a mosquito between his fingertips and began to sweat.

He had not failed today, and it gave him a feeling of satisfaction. He had been commandant of Emga during a battle. Excitement, worries and a little fear. But now it was over. He had become older but his ambition was still very much alive. Once the war was over he would embellish the story. He could hear himself saying: "Within four hours the Russians overran the division. The front line had gone. There was terrible disorder. Then I received orders from the Army to halt the retreat. He need not go into too many details. He would omit the story of the car which had stood outside waiting to take him away. He wiped the sweat from his forehead with a dirty handkerchief and at this moment he looked exactly like a gnome. As soon as the cavalry captain came in and sat down in the chair the major came to the point.

"What's happened to the sergeant major?"

The captain thought for a second and said, "Nothing." Although he had not yet had any dealings with the commandant he felt that this interview would take an unpleasant turn.

"You don't seem to have understood me. I gave you an order. When do you propose to carry it out?"

"Never." Shocked at his own boldness the captain added: "He's had no trial."

This was a bad start. The major seemed purposely to ignore the word "never." "It's a complicated case," he said. "The judge advocate was a fool. We two have to suffer the consequences."

"Excuse me, Herr Major, but I don't quite understand why." The light from the lamp blinded the captain. A moth was fluttering around the lamp chimney.

The commandant began to give a long-winded explanation. "The army wanted to hold someone up as an example and it had to be a severe one. Everything was touch-and-go. They wanted to warn the troops by giving them a horrifying example. A similar mess can happen again tomorrow. Possibly the judge advocate was incorrectly informed. He was sent to Emga to carry out an execution. It did not matter whom he picked, only it should not have been an ordinary soldier. Who could I have chosen? You perhaps."

The captain felt that he was turning red. "So you chose the sergeant major and gave his name to the army. The army circulated the information that the sergeant major had been shot. In the meanwhile the judge advocate condemned the wrong man to death and the sergeant major is still alive. A tragedy without a corpse."

"It's our duty to deliver the corpse."

The captain pushed his chair a little to the side, for the light from the lamp was becoming unbearable. Each time the moth hit its wings against the hot globe it tinkled softly. "That's crazy," he said.

The major frowned. "The man was obviously a deserter."

"We could have found thousands of them." The captain thought of his driver. The bastard who had left him behind.

The commandant wrinkled his forehead. "According to information received so far we have suffered four thousand casualties, either dead or taken prisoner. The sergeant major's company for example has been practically wiped out. One more or less makes no difference."

"That's just the point, Major."

"What more do you want? Theoretically the man is dead. His next of kin will have been informed and he has been written off the rolls. His pay book has been cancelled.

What is more, the various company commanders must have already read the army dispatch giving details of the execution."

"A most unfortunate circular," said the captain. The globe tinkled. The moth was firmly resolved to die.

"And everything depends upon this most unfortunate circular as you call it."

"And suppose we gave him the chance to desert?"

The major shook his head. "How could you do it? If the sergeant major isn't shot, there'll be a stink. One day people will start making inquiries and insist upon my producing the body. Like a sort of receipt. Then what do we do?"

"As commandant you have certain possibilities." The major shook his head. "I'm no longer commandant. The break-through has been sealed off." Suddenly he banged his fist on the table and shouted: "What you propose is high treason." In his anger he swept one of the many pencils from the table. He had a collector's weakness for pencils. "You'll shoot him," he ordered.

The globe tinkled. The moth fell to the floor. Its burnt wings were still quivering.

"Order the military police to do it," suggested the captain.

The major bent down to pick up the pencil and bobbed up again. "The M.P. could refuse. He knows that there has been no sentence." He gave an unpleasant smile. "There is a difference you know between you and the M.P. He has a clean slate." There was a painful silence. The whirr of a mosquito which had taken the moth's place around the lamp was the only noise in the room.

"How is that?" asked the captain slowly.

"I have proof that your detachment retired from its position without reason. A report from me and you're finished."

The sweat broke out on the captain's forehead. He had made a mistake. Now he remembered. He should have destroyed the time table. The entries could now prove what had happened. The town commandant had a radio receiving post where all incoming message were registered together with the time. Probably one of the radio operators of his sector had reported: "No contact with the enemy." And he had retreated at that particular moment. In the orders were written: Under enemy pressure retire to point X. The fellow had known this the whole time.

"Well?" asked the major.

"Do you gurantee me . . ."

The commandant laughed genially.

"May I go now?"

"Yes. And—report back to me when you have carried out my order."

In the corridor which led to the courtyard the captain felt like a diver walking on firm ground with leaden plates on his feet. The courtyard lay in darkness. A dull murmur came from the front. The barn loomed up ahead of him like an enormous ship. Involuntarily he slowed his steps.

In an hour he would be a murderer and, if things went quickly, in half an hour. It was a rotten business—like a bad play. He sat in a box looking onto the stage. Suddenly he was to take part in it. As a spectator he would not have found this difficult but as the time for his entrance drew near he became more and more nervous. Must he really go ahead? Yes. There was that time table. A harmless strip of paper; a devilish contract. If he got out of it cheaply he would lose his rank . . .

A car engine droned in the darkness. Two tiny lights groped over the square. The darkened headlights looked like All Souls candles flickering in a cemetery. A pair of boots crunched on the gravel. Suddenly he stood before the closed iron door of the barn. He knocked. The iron resounded like a drum.

"Come on in," said the M.P. as though it were a dinner party. A miner's lamp hung on the wall and threw jagged shadows on the table. It could not have made the barn look more dreary. A spider's web hung in the air and brushed against his face. When he rubbed it away he felt a spider on his hand and shuddered with disgust. Huge patches of the plaster had fallen from the walls and he had to make his way across the debris. White patches of wall like the sheets in a morgue, hung out to dry. "Is it all set?" the M.P. whispered, like a conspirator.

The captain shook his head. So I'm to be spared nothing, he thought. The man will remember my face. Apart from myself and the major there's now a third party who knows about the affair. Only now did he begin to understand the monstrosity of the proceedings.

"The commandant told me you would be coming to fetch him," whispered the M.P.

"Why don't you speak out loud!" asked the captain.

"Hush!" The M.P. put his forefinger to his lips. "He's out." He pointed upwards into the darkness.

The captain repeated it at first without comprehending and then with pleasure. "He's out." This was the best thing he had heard so far. He giggled. He had always known that it was only a bad joke. The sergeant major had gone. This was the only possibility upon which he had not reckoned. He laughed aloud: he was a frustrated hangman. The business with the time-table would also be straightened out.

"Shh—the sergeant major's asleep," the M.P. hissed.

The captain felt as though someone had thrown a pail of cold water in his face. "Explain yourself more clearly," he stammered.

"He's asleep," replied the M.P., offended. He went on, business-like: "I'd like to keep his revolver. And you must sign the receipt, here."

"Receipt?"

"According to regulations I have to have a receipt when I hand over a prisoner." Cold shivers ran down the captain's spine and he dug his nails into his palms. Finally the major would be asking for the man's ears by way of proof. The M.P. handed him a tattered book. "Sign here please."

"Later, later," growled the captain. A murderer does not leave his name behind.

"But he's still alive," said the M.P., obviously disappointed.

The captain saw a steep stair opening into the darkness. Rotting planks, cement dust and a ricketty bannister. I must climb up, he thought. He is asleep. How can a man sleep when he is going to die?

The M.P.'s voice interrupted his thoughts. "It might be more unpleasant later when it's all over."

The captain fell silent. The shot would give a powerful echo in this old building. The flame of the explosion would light up the whole barn. Perhaps he would miss and the sergeant major would then begin to scream. And suppose it came to a struggle. In the face of death man is capable of anything.

"If you don't give me a light, I can't find him in the dark," he said in reproach.

"I'll fetch him."

"No, no! If he's asleep . . ."

The M.P. was at a loss. "But we must wake him anyway."

"I'll do it while he's asleep," said the captain hastily. "That's the best way."

"It can't be done."

"Does that mean I have to do it outside?"

He purposely avoided saying the words "shoot him."

"Yes. Those are the major's orders."

"How does he think I'm going to do it?" stammered the captain. "What shall I say to the sergeant major?"

"Hush! Not so loud! I've told him he's to be released tomorrow. I do that with all of them."

The captain was amazed at this indifference. "Well, go and fetch him then." A cold sweat stood on his forehead. There was no turning back now. The flame of the miner's lamp flickered like a will-o'-the-wisp.

The M.P. climbed up the stairs and the planks creaked under his footsteps. A bunch of keys rattled. The door squeaked unpleasantly. In the darkness a strip of plaster came loose from the wall and fell with a thud to the floor. It made the captain jump. Overhead he could hear an indistinct murmur. A second voice broke in and then there was movement. A man got up, sleepily. The floor above creaked and steps came down the stairs. The bannister began to tremble.

"You're to be transferred," heard the captain.

"Here he is," said a voice at his side and the sergeant major stood in front of him. The captain stared at the white wall patches.

"My watch," he heard the sergeant major say.

"I haven't got it," replied the M.P.

"But it's gone!"

"Don't get smart!" barked the M.P.

The captain thought he had never witnessed anything more monstrous in his life. He knew who had the watch. The M.P. made it only too obvious.

"And my belt and revolver?" asked the sergeant major.

"They will remain here," replied the captain in a voice that he himself did not recognize.

"Wouldn't you rather do it now?" said the M.P. holding out the tattered book once more.

"No, later! Let's get going!"

The captain felt relieved once he was clear of the lantern light. While the M.P. opened the iron door the sergeant major complained: "Without a belt?" This struck the captain as laughable. As they stepped outside, the roar from the front line sounded like the din at a railway shunting station. A red glow rose above the woods. Their footsteps rang out in the darkness.

The captain suddenly felt afraid. It seemed to him as though the sergeant major was purposely keeping behind him. In the excitement he fumbled for his revolver holster and opened the flap. He felt the cold steel and took out the weapon. He was sure that the sergeant major had not noticed his movements. Yet he could not get rid of his fear although with his weapon he had the upper hand. Then it suddenly entered his head that the safety catch was on. It was impossible to remove it without making a click. The sergeant major would hear it. A new abyss yawned . . . The man would then know that his murderer was walking at his side or else he would immediately decide to flee. Isn't anyone coming, thought the captain. He longed to hear some voice even if it were only that of a stranger. This being alone with his victim was unbearable. And where should he do it? This was also an open question. The forest was not far away but he simply could not bring himself to go into the forest alone with the sergeant major. The trees, the thicket, the branches which hung like ghosts over the path and the darkness.

"It's time I rejoined my company," said the sergeant major. He was still a pace behind the captain. Was it cunning or military discipline? The fear of death makes one childish. While the captain was thinking out his reply the sergeant major asked: "Where are we going, Captain?"

The captain had known subconsciously that this question was coming and yet it caught him unawares. He had never before had to think out a lie so quickly, at least not such a significant lie.

"There are a few formalities," he said thinking that by now he must have betrayed himself.

"I need a certification of the time that I have been here. Otherwise my company will really think that . . ." The sergeant major's voice had a demanding undertone.

At this moment the captain removed the safety catch. It surprised himself. He had done it instinctively while the man was speaking. He himself could not understand this cold-bloodedness. Now he had removed all barriers that led to the murder. A mere pressure of his fingers. But what would happen if he missed? They had crossed the courtyard and were approaching a house. A duck board lay in their path and the captain stumbled over it. He dropped the revolver and it tinkled in the darkness against a stone. It was a miracle that it did not go off

"Your weapon," said the sergeant major.

The captain did not reply but began to grope feverishly

about the ground. The sharp gravel tore his hands. Once he thought he had found it but it was only a flat piece of iron.

"Perhaps it's over here," said the sergeant major bending down.

At that moment the captain thought he would scream. He could not bear this a moment longer. "Never mind," he stammered but the sergeant major was already crawling about on the ground. Their hands touched. "Let me look for it," implored the officer.

"I've got it," said the sergeant major standing up. The captain remained squatting there, completely exhausted. He saw the gigantic shadow of the sergeant major looming above him. There was a pressure around his heart. This is the end, he thought, waiting for the shot. A fraction of a second. An eternity.

"Here you are," said the sergeant major.

What is the next move? thought the captain. His legs refused to function.

"Here you are, Captain."

He stretched out his hand, touched the other man's hand and felt the barrel of the revolver. The muzzle was pointing at his belly and the weapon was ready for firing. The slightest pressure and he would die. "It's cocked," he wanted to say. When the butt was finally in his hand he felt like a drunken man. The courtyard and the house all seemed to be swaying. "We must get going," he whispered. There were huts on both sides of the road, small black, pointed boxes. The captain had no idea where they should go.

"Have I got to reckon with a punishment?" asked the sergeant major suddenly growing suspicious. "You have to reckon with everything here," he said with an embarrassed laugh.

The huts now lay behind them and they had reached a stretch which belonged to the station. A mountain of coal stacked ready for the engines. The skeleton of a burned out railroad car. Somewhere away to the right, out of sight, water splashed into a container. The captain could feel gravel and then railway tracks under his feet. He was surprised to hear himself answer: "I'll not keep you in suspense any longer. Things look pretty grim for you." He spoke very quietly. "Your head's in the balance. The Army has demanded the ultimate penalty."

The sergeant major stopped short, terrified. He was panting. "I thought they were letting me go back to my company."

"The M.P. lied to you."

"That is . . ." stammered the sergeant major. "No! No. . . ."

The captain could sense his terror. "Disappear!" he shouted. "Start running, man! Run for your life! I can't do more than that for you. Perhaps you can get to the Russian lines. Start running!"

For a moment everything was silent. The sergeant major's breathing grew leaden and then he took hold of himself. The captain saw the shadow and heard his victim's footsteps on the gravel. He thought of the time-table, of the fatal entry. Then he fired. Once. Twice. His fingers pressed the trigger and the shots lashed the air. The sergeant major gave a faint scream and by the light of the shots he saw him collapse. The captain went on pressing the trigger. Greed, fear and rage guided his hand. An empty click. He had fired all his bullets. He flung the weapon away in disgust. Tears ran down his face. He turned around and staggered away.

"A bath," he whispered. Suddenly he shouted it—"I must take a bath!" And with these words he left the realms of sanity. Until his death it was maintained that the barrage had driven him mad.

Epilogue

THREE days later a cold wind blowing in from the sea, sucked up the warmth from the forest. The marshes began to steam and fog hung over the low lying ground. The swarms of mosquitoes had disappeared and there was a tang of autumn in the air.

In the mist that swirled a foot above the ground a few soldiers stood at the edge of an open grave in the Podrowa cemetery. They had collected their dead and brought them to be buried. A priest who a few days ago had still been preaching in a real church performed the ceremony with great zeal. He had arrived with the fresh troops at the front. In his bewilderment at what he found there he devoted himself to duties which a few weeks later he would hand over to a layman. One of these duties was this burial service. He placed his stole on his shoulders, took a small crucifix from his breast and opened his field Bible.

"God be with you," he began. His attention was focused partly on the soldiers and partly on the words of the holy scripture. The faces of the soldiers reminded him of those chill, expressionless stone ornaments that stare down at you from graves. It would be difficult for him to reach their hearts.

"For ever and ever. Amen" he said aloud. He noticed the major wearing no boots, his feet wrapped in sacking. White bandages gleamed beneath the brown material. He could not recognize the face for the man was staring into the grave.

"My dear brothers in Christ," he said unctuously. "This is a sad occasion on which we plead for God's presence. We have lost our comrades. The Lord in his wisdom has willed it so." He had long ago decided that he would say this were he faced with such an event. "Good is too great," he went on, "for us to be able to divine His plans. The Lord calls and we must obey. He is wise and omniscient. We must believe without understanding." A sergeant who was looking exceedingly bored near the edge of the forest, and who was obviously not listening, distracted his attention. "Without understanding," he repeated. Then he remembered what he was going to say. "Look at the sky above us; it is majestic and powerful. Look at the clouds up there. What are we compared with them? We are but small and insignificant creatures." A runner with a dispatch case caught his eye. He was the only one who had no new medals on his tunic, as though for some reason he had been absent when they had been distributed. "Bear your sorrows with humility," went on the priest. "Do not ask God why one has been taken and the other left. For the Lord is silent. Only when we have returned to ashes will He come and say 'There will be light' and this is our consolation. . . ."

The major turned to the sergeant. "I must go. My feet. It's so damned cold."

The sergeant nodded. "Lean on me, Major. I'll help you."

Thoughtfully they left the cemetery. The soldiers made way for them smartly. After they had gone a few steps the sergeant said: "You mustn't think I'm particularly pleased to leave that service. It rings so pleasantly in your ears. It's something different. Besides . . . secretly we all hope it's true."

"Yes," replied the major. "It would be unthinkable if that were a lie too."